Fourth Attempt

Elite Escorts 1

Lynn Burke

Fourth Attempt

Wren Shipman is not my usual leggy blonde, but she ensnares me. Tilts my world off its axis.

At my first attempt to ask her out, she claims a wealthy, arrogant playboy isn't her type—an accurate judgment according to my social media.

But I only want her.

At my second attempt, she claims she's too busy earning her college degree to refine the stain of her poor upbringing.

But I already see her as perfect.

In vulnerable desperation, I make a third attempt to show her I'm hoping for more than just another notch on my bedpost.

I end up in the friend zone and fall even harder for the woman who is everything I'm not.

When bitter reality threatens Wren's dreams of graduating, I jump at the opportunity to reveal I have depth beyond what she assumes.

Will she give me a chance to prove I'm trustworthy...or will she break the heart she refuses to believe she owns?

Chapter 1

Wren

I climbed from my old Chevy Lumina, the muggy atmosphere immediately prickling my skin with the need to sweat. Early July, and wicked summer weather already haunted Massachusetts, causing flowers and maple leaves alike to droop.

Attempting to fill my lungs with the swamp-like air and yanking my bag over my shoulder, I slammed the squeaky driver door shut and took a quick perusal of the half-built monstrosity on the lot behind me.

The daily noise of power tools and nail guns didn't bother me. The fact the condo building would eventually rise higher than my third-floor apartment in the old Victorian house and cut off my view of the Merrimac River?

Yeah. I wasn't happy about that fact, but I was in no place financially to move.

One good thing about the construction that started up a few weeks ago? Countless muscled men to fuel my imagination and give me something to fantasize about since real life working the night shift at a pharmacy sucked.

But because of work and college courses, I also had no time or emotional capacity to get involved, no matter how much I yearned for someone to hold me. Support me. Encourage me when my energy ran low—like it always seemed to do.

So, I simply focused on the best part I couldn't keep my eyes off of.

The driver of the new silver F-250 with Harper's Construction painted on its side.

Blake Harper in all his six-foot-plus glory climbed from the cab a stone's toss away, and same as always when I caught a glimpse of the man, I swallowed a moan and a rush of drool.

The size of his pristine work boots suggested he was no small boy where it counted. His tight jeans hugged him in all the right places, leaving nothing to the imagination, and implied the same thing his feet hinted at.

Perspiration beaded between my breasts as I allowed myself to linger beneath the scorching sun in order to soak in the sight of physical perfection.

His navy button-down with the construction logo over his thick left pec hadn't yet been dirtied from the day's work and still appeared starched to perfection. I doubted he laundered his own clothes, but with the money he came from, why would he? The sleeves were rolled to his elbow, his thick, muscular forearms the type I dreamed of having wrapped around me, comforting and erasing all the burdens from my mind.

Light brown hair that appeared too carefully mussed topped his tall form, and blond highlights on the tips glinting in the sun made my fingers ache to grasp and hold on tight. Slashed eyebrows, a clean-shaven, sharp jawline, and cheekbones to die for made him runway worthy and the leading man in my dreams. Full lips with a perfect bow suggested he knew how to use his mouth to drug a woman with sensual kisses I'd never truly experienced and absolutely *ached* for. Dark blue eyes fringed by thick, dark lashes—

His focus landed on me, stealing my thoughts and breath.

Blake was a damn magnetic field stronger than any science fiction tractor beam. A wave of electrical current reached out across the short distance between us, attempting to snag hold of me. Ensnare me. Make me powerless...

I *couldn't* move beneath his perusal.

His gaze caressed over me like X-ray vision, allowing him to peer through the wrinkled pharmacy uniform hiding my boyish figure I'd always hated. I could feel his appraisal like erotic feathering fingertips beneath my clothing. Shivers slid over my heated skin.

Damp panties? Check.

Tight nipples aching for teeth? Double check.

Our gazes once more connected—his slow, cocky smile snapped me back to reality even though my pulse continued to thrum in my neck. Those midnight blues stated he knew how the mere sight of him affected my body.

My chin lifted as I attempted to sniff down my nose at him. The arrogant ass was *so* not my type, I told myself, even if he did look like a Greek god.

According to social media, Blake had his pick of women and wasn't shy about flashing those pictures to brag. He liked them tall and graceful, blonde from a bottle, and with enough makeup caked on their faces to keep Sephora in business.

The opposite of me.

A true playboy bachelor, he also never got photographed with a woman more than once.

Not that I stalked him or anything. I wasn't interested in his life even if he *did* make my body purr. And I *definitely* wasn't looking for a romp in the sheets that would leave me swooning over a man who refused to be tied down. Blake would be just like all of Mom's boyfriends who'd been in and out of our lives as fast as a synodic day.

Nope. Nuh uh.

I'd had more than enough of those types during my childhood—except for the rich part. Trusting a man to actually stick around and make all my happily-ever-after dreams come true wasn't going to happen no matter how pretty or wealthy he was.

Without returning Blake's knowing smile, I spun and trudged up the exterior stairs to my apartment, a small one-bedroom on the third floor/attic of a house that had seen better days. I yanked open the wooden door that had swelled with the humidity, but the scent of fresh coffee along with a blast of AC in my face eased the growl of annoyance rising in my chest.

Same as every morning, I thanked the gods that some human thought up a timer so I didn't have to stand and twiddle my thumbs while waiting for the coffee to finish brewing.

Two sugars and a splash of cream went into my steaming mug, and I sat at my small table beside the window overlooking the river through framed floors of the building across the street.

It wouldn't be long before a brick exterior blocked off the peaceful view I'd enjoyed for the couple of years I'd lived there.

With a perfect scene of the toiling men below, I sipped and grieved the fact they would eventually be gone too.

The racket of building filtered through the glass, but I didn't mind since it didn't compare to the shithole I'd grown up in.

My attention glued to Blake and who I assumed to be his foreman, a slightly shorter, dark-haired gorgeous guy I enjoyed watching boss around the other employees when the cocky asshole wasn't on site.

Blake held a set of rolled blueprints under one arm as the two men walked around, pointing at this or that and chatting with the carpenters. After their morning tour of the site, which lasted through my first cup of coffee, the two men headed into the trailer office alongside the road. I had to lean forward to keep them in sight until the door shut behind them.

Coming Soon the big red sign beside the office at the construction site's entrance read, *Werner's Point, Luxury Condos.*

Private parking, docks for those with boats, and balconies overlooking the river soon to be stolen from me, the website promised. Well, the owner didn't give a shit about the last part, but no one ever cared what happened to those who came before the new, moneymaking condo buildings sprouted up.

Sighing over losing sight of my favorite fantasy man, I retrieved a second cup of coffee and returned to my seat. My gaze once more lifted to the river lazing its way toward the Atlantic Ocean.

One day, I would be out of debt and rise above the label of white trash from Lynn, the City of Sin, as it was called. Sure, I'd moved from where my mom had raised me—and where she still wallowed. The stink of my childhood clung to my nostrils and skin regardless of the raspberry lotion I slathered on every inch of my body after showering.

Like the river, slow and steady, I had studied my ass off and worked my way out of that place. Daily, I thanked every god and saint imaginable that I'd been blessed with a measure of intelligence from my father since my mom had zero brains to speak of. He'd been the supposed love of my mom's life who had lasted longer than the rest of her men.

They'd spent a whole whopping week together.

In reality, he'd been nothing more than a sperm donor, leaving Mom twenty-five years earlier without a trace of his existence other than the cleft in my chin. Beyond that single physical trait? I looked just like my mom.

Mousy brown hair that never caught the sunlight with auburn or golden glints like Blake's thick locks. Some might appreciate my hazel-brown irises, but they hid behind glasses since contacts dried my eyes out to the point of pain.

Mom and I were both petite with a serious lack of curves, but at least I didn't have track marks littering my arms or premature wrinkles from choosing to party rather than take care of myself.

While I didn't respect her for falling into drugs and having dozens of boyfriends throughout my childhood, I appreciated the roof she'd kept over our heads and the food in my belly by working countless part-time jobs. She'd never once raised her hand toward me in anger, but she also never offered her arms for comfort or affection either.

She hadn't been around that much and left me to my own devices, but at least no one had called the police on her where I'd have been tossed into the system. It was no wonder I'd become independent at an early age, determined to make more of myself than she had chosen to do.

But I also found myself touch starved.

The two guys I had dated had quickly grown tired of my neediness, my clinging onto them every chance I'd been gifted.

No one wanted a leech.

Especially one with a childhood as tarnished as mine.

Rubbing at my tired eyes beneath my glasses, I let out a heavy sigh, exhaling away thoughts of the ashes I was determined to rise above.

I swallowed down the last of my coffee and hit the shower, ready for my summer class to be over so I could crash for a few hours of sleep.

In ten months, six years of schooling would be a part of my past, and I would be a licensed pharmacist, making the pay that would eventually afford me a condo like the ones being built across the street.

I lathered up my hair, my eyes shut and mind dreaming beneath the tepid stream of water. One day, I would be debt free and finally feel a sense of satisfaction with my life.

Maybe I would get lucky and find an affectionate man who couldn't keep his hands off me...one as hot as Blake Harper without the self-entitlement he portrayed online.

Snorting, I shut that fantasy down before the lonely little girl inside me went all heart-eyed over imagining soft kisses and warm arms to hold me tight.

Affirmations of love and acceptance—they'd all been proven false in my past, so what was the point of hoping or relying on others to fill me up with happiness?

Head set on straight and ready to get my ass to class, I went back out into the heat, hurried down my stairs, and hopped into my piece-of-shit car without once glancing across the street.

Regardless of my yearnings for intimacy, it was best to

stay focused on the one person I could rely on to provide for my future.

Me.

Chapter 2

Blake

Prime building time was in early July, and my head threatened to explode from sinus pressure. I couldn't breathe because of the elephant-like heaviness sitting on my chest. Didn't sleep worth a shit all weekend because my aching body couldn't get comfortable.

Dragging my ass out of bed on Monday morning, I grabbed the closest shirt off my bedroom floor, too fucking out of it to care what it was or if the damn thing was even clean.

I attempted to sniff for BO, but what a crock of shit that was too with how my nose was clogged up like a toilet stuffed full of paper. Soft cotton instead of starched draped over my torso, and I didn't even look in the mirror before forcing myself to get in the truck.

Not long after sunrise, bleary-eyed, blinking, and yawning so hard my ears popped, I decided I'd had enough of toughing it out.

A pharmacy sat close by the jobsite, so I swung into the nearly empty parking lot.

I needed the daytime clear-up-your-fucking-head-and-take-the-throbbing-away-so-you-can-get-shit-done type of medicine before I showed up for work.

I stood in the cold and flu aisle, rubbing my palm over the scruff lining my jaw while staring, my brain half dead from the lack of sleep. Couldn't even remember walking into the damn drugstore.

Muffled music reached through the fluff in my ears, but I couldn't make out the words or tune. Didn't even bother trying.

Dozens of cold medicine brands lined the shelves in purple, red, and green boxes. I picked up one of each color. They all listed drugs I couldn't pronounce or begin to guess at how they would help me.

"Fuck." My stuffy murmur echoed inside my pounding head. I grabbed two other boxes and headed to the pharmacy counter at the back of the store. "'Scuse me?"

A tiny woman, head bent with honey-brown hair hiding her face, counted out pills on a tray.

"Be right with you," she mumbled without glancing my way.

So tired I couldn't even blink, I let the boxes tumble from my arms onto the counter so I could lean my palms against it to hold me up.

She poured the pills into an amber bottle, twisted on a childproof cap, and slapped a label around it.

"What can I help you with?" she asked, starting toward me. Her focus lifted, eyes widening behind the nerdy glasses perched on her petite nose.

She didn't have that hot librarian thing going on with tits spilling out of a low-cut blouse, but something about her in the unflattering, scrubs-like outfit she wore snagged my full focus and woke me up the slightest bit.

I actually smiled at the flutters in my stomach like I was

some lovesick middle schooler seeing his crush in the school's hallway.

The fuck?

No woman had done that to me. Ever. Not even the one person I had allowed—

Pushing aside the thoughts I refused to dwell on, I took in the beguiling woman in front of me.

Pink tinted her cheeks, a gorgeous flush that warmed my chest and made me wish I'd been the one to put it there.

She stood no taller than my pecs—pint-sized. And damn cute too.

Clearing her throat, she glanced down at the medicine I'd dumped on the counter. "I'm guessing you have a cold?"

I couldn't help but stare down at her, my insides a riotous mess. "Yeah."

"Fever?"

"Nah. Just stuffed up. Pretty sure my head is going to pop before I get a chance to down some much needed coffee."

Leaving the boxes on the counter, she pushed through a waist-high swinging door and motioned me to follow her back the way I'd come. Not that I needed prodding. I gravitated toward her on instinct, my gaze dropping to her backside. Her shirt hung past her ass, not nearly tight enough for me to get a hint at what lay beneath.

My hands would span her waist, I didn't doubt, and all that long, wavy hair gathered in a low ponytail begged for my fist to tip her head so I could ravish her neck with teeth-grazing kisses.

Life twitched in my groin at the thought of loving all over her body until she lay spent beneath me.

I couldn't smell a damn thing thanks to my cold, but I imagined she'd be sweet in my nose.

She drew up in front of the shelf I'd been staring at, and fuck, how I wanted to crowd in tight against her and see what her ass felt like pressed all over my front. She was so short—

Squatting rather than bending for my viewing pleasure, she pulled a box off the bottom shelf. "That'll clear you up for the day."

She turned and smiled up at me with a guarded expression I wasn't used to seeing on the opposite sex. Not a stitch of makeup highlighted her face. Full but pale lips and porcelain skin most women would kill for created natural beauty—the kind I wouldn't mind marking with my teeth.

The desire to slip off her glasses, bite those lips, and wrap my hands around her throat slid through my sluggish brain and blood, and my cock stirred a little more despite my feeling like shit.

Usually, I would drop a line or two, make my dimple pop, and not bother beating around the bush about my intentions, but I was too woolly-headed and addled from the feelings inside me to think straight let alone flirt or ask her out.

I took the box from her hand without a word. Our fingertips brushed, shooting a zing up my arm and straight down to my dick. Those were some serious sparks, and I swallowed a groan.

Her large hazel eyes widened, mouth parted on a fast exhale as though she'd felt the same impending explosion.

I narrowed my gaze in concentration, wracking my foggy brain as I realized she looked familiar. There was no way I'd fucked her. I would never forget the woman who was unlike my usual hookups. She was shrimp-sized, the type a guy my size could carry around all day without growing tired.

The thought of her tiny body wrapped around me, heels clinging to my ass and mouth sucking on my neck, sent a shot of adrenaline and rush of lust to my groin, waking me up to the point my pants grew uncomfortable.

"I've seen you before," I murmured, my voice far from flirtatious and sexy with its stuffy tone.

She nodded, her cheeks still pink, but she held my gaze like a damn champ for how shy she seemed. "You own Harper's Construction."

My head tipped to the side as I studied her hazel orbs half-hidden by those sexy glasses, wondering why she didn't get that calculating glint in her eye most women did when they figured out who I was. The money I had. What I could give them.

"Yeah," I answered, baffled and intrigued as fuck.

The fuck has she done to me?

Maybe it was the cold. Stuffed head. I wasn't thinking straight.

Her chin with the cutest dimple lifted, shoulders pulling back as though offended rather than impressed by whose attention she'd completely ensnared. "I live across from what will be Werner's Point."

Memory hit me.

The young woman who'd snagged my eyes the Friday before. I'd only caught a glimpse of her before she'd turned and strode away without the usual backward glance I got more often than not from men and women alike.

"Blake Harper." I held out my hand even though she seemed less than thrilled to officially meet the man who would block her apartment's view of the river.

She peered at my outstretched offering long enough I

shifted on my feet in a rare outward display of...something I felt clear through my bones. Tilted off my axis, I peered at the small woman who shouldn't have been able to unsettle me.

But definitely had.

Unease had my feet moving slightly again. Couldn't fucking help it. The woman, in the brief span of minutes, had somehow burrowed into me like a damn tick.

I *had* to get her under me so I could pluck her from beneath my skin and move on.

With a huffed exhale, she finally clasped my hand.

Talk about a lightning strike straight to the dick. I flinched hard, my abs going tight as fuck as I swallowed a groan. Such a small hand. Soft. Slender. I wanted those fingers stroking through my hair, worshiping every muscle lining my upper body and attempting to grasp around my dick.

Fuck.

I swallowed hard as the earth quaked beneath my feet. I was so damn off my game—

"Wren Shipman," she stated, that firm lift of her chin still in place as though she looked down her nose at me.

Laughable with her size, really, but her backbone only enticed me all the more.

"Wren? As in the bird?" I managed the smirk that revealed the dimple women loved.

The pink in her cheeks deepened, returning some of my confidence when faced with something I wanted. Lusted for. Had to have.

"Yes."

Fuck, did I love hearing that word on her lips.

Pretty, pretty bird...I'm going to enjoy every second of ruffling your feathers.

Chapter 3

Wren

My heart pounded in my ears and my knees weakened at Blake's firm hand wrapped around mine. At the obvious lust in his eyes, I put on my *I'm not interested in being one of your bedpost notches* look.

Cool and clinical. Unfazed and disinterested.

Or, so I hoped I appeared that way.

But oh, my insides—hell, *everything* inside me wanted to lean into him. Sniff. Snuggle. Worship. Lick. Maybe even nibble a bit if he enjoyed a little scraping of teeth over his skin. He smelled like man and sleepy warmth, soap and dryer sheets, and I wanted to curl up beneath the blanket of his god-like body.

Shutting down those thoughts, I pulled my hand from his and pointed toward the front of the store before he could make a fool of himself by asking me out. There was no point in his trying to weasel his way into my panties and attempt another conquest over the closest female.

He would fail. Period.

"Beth will ring you up, Mr. Harper," I said. "I hope

you're feeling better soon and get some rest." Without waiting for a reply, I hightailed it back behind the pharmacy counter as though the fire on my backside was really flames rather than his steady gaze.

Jenny, the third shift pharmacist, scrolled through her cell in the small room she mixed compounds in. I stepped into the nook and closed the door within an inch of latching, leaving just enough of a crack for me to watch the sexy-as-hell playboy head to the storefront.

He'd been even more intimidating...luscious-looking...*hotter* all up in my personal space. Not one damn imperfection marred his face. Not. One.

"Criminal," I murmured with a sigh, sagging against the doorframe to hold me steady, since he'd made me shiver and shake from hair to toenails. I couldn't catch my damn breath, and I hadn't even been exercising.

It was a wonder I hadn't swooned at his big feet, putting my face right where I could easily find out what he hid inside those work pants. He would have let me too, I didn't doubt.

I wasn't well-schooled in the art of seduction, had only been on the receiving end of it twice in my life, but I recognized desire in his dark blues that tempted me to go all weak-kneed like most women probably did when he flashed his smile and that sexy-as-hell dimple.

Damn man.

But why me? I had no idea since I was pretty much a munchkin and had no curves to speak of—

"What are you up to?" Jenny asked, her voice startling me back to reality.

I'd forgotten where I stood...what I was supposed to be doing. My eyes and mind had been ensnared by the gravitational pull of the hottest guy I'd ever seen.

"Salivating over the most delicious man ever," I muttered the absolute truth of Blake Harper. All sexy swagger and rumpled clothing...mussed hair and stubble lining his jawline.

Jenny leaned around me and pushed the door open a bit wider.

I crouched down enough she could see over my head. Easily done since she stood five-foot-ten to my less than five.

Up at the store's front counter, Blake flustered Beth if her red face and gaping mouth gave any indication of his effect on her.

Did he shamelessly flirt? Or was it merely the sight of his perfection that made Beth look like she needed to fan her face?

God knew I felt the same over the man who appeared as though he'd just crawled out of bed after satisfying a woman.

A flash of jealousy curdled my stomach, pulling my eyebrows into a frown. I snorted. *Get over yourself and enjoy the view.*

My gaze roamed across his broad shoulders stretching out his tight T-shirt to his round backside hugged by those... construction-type pants.

"God, he's got an ass," Jenny murmured above me.

I moaned my agreement.

Round and tight, perfect for wrapping my legs around. The thought sent flickers of heat kissing along my thighs, but hundreds of women had without a doubt done that very thing while sinking their fake nails into his back.

No thank you.

"I'd do him for free." Jenny sighed as Blake glanced

back our way before walking out the exit, the automatic door swishing shut behind him.

I sagged from the adrenaline crash. "Along with every other hot guy to waltz in here like he's some god's gift to women," I reminded Jenny, pushing open the door we'd hidden behind.

"So many men, so little hours in a day." Her snicker brought a smile to my face.

I'd heard that one from her mouth a hundred or so times in the two years we'd worked the night shift together.

"Doubling up on occasion would help me get through my to-do list," she mused another thought she'd mentioned before.

A puff of laughter huffed from me as I went back to the delivery order I'd been filling when Blake's "'Scuse me" had woken me from daydreaming about him. I'd nearly swallowed my tongue when I looked up and found him peering at me with those dreamy blue eyes.

And those lips...

It was like my subconscious had called out to him through time and space, drawing him into the pharmacy just to knock my knees and steal my breath.

Hot damn.

I shook my head, enjoying yet hating how heat dampened my panties at the thought of his kisses, his large hands all over my body. Loving on me like no man had ever done. Like I was his sole focus, the reason his heart beat.

"Ever have a threesome?" Jenny asked, tearing my brain from its wandering.

"Nope. Have you?"

"Once, my sophomore year in college." Jenny sighed again. "Then three guys at the same time my senior year. It was the best damn night of my life. Mouths, fingers, and dicks everywhere."

"Seriously?" I glanced over my shoulder to find her eyes hazed and face flushed.

"All those men, their full attention plastered on me...oh, hell yeah."

The thought of Blake Harper alone brought about fantasies that rocked my world, but throwing another man into the mix? My entire body heated as the memory of his foreman's face flashed across my mind. Dark hair and eyes like sinful chocolate, he was the opposite of Blake yet just as gorgeous. Having all that attention and affection at once?

Couldn't. Even. Imagine.

"Now a man like *that*," Jenny said, "you can tell by how he walks he knows his way around the female body. I'll bet he wouldn't need help satisfying a woman's needs."

Jenny's words flitted through my ears, bringing to attention the fact he'd probably done more women than all of Hollywood's leading men combined.

Again with the no thank you.

"You can have him," I stated firmly, grabbing a bottle of antidepressants off the shelf.

ℋℋ

Later that morning, I climbed out of my car and rounded my downstairs neighbor's SUV while stifling a yawn, proud of myself for not even glancing across the street.

Blake sat on the bottom step of my exterior stairs.

I stumbled to a stop, my heart skipping a beat at the grin on his face. He held two Dunks coffees in his large hands, elbows resting on his knees.

"Good morning," he said, his eyes clearer and more alert than they'd been earlier at the pharmacy.

The breath punched from my lungs. My mouth's drool factory went on high alert, alarms blaring and everything.

Still damn luscious-looking, Blake was even more panty-melting with the husky rasp in his tone no longer hidden by congestion. Goddamn him for being outwardly perfect in every way. It was seriously unfortunate his insides didn't match what peered at me.

"How's the cold?" I asked without returning his smile or the greeting. The only good thing about mornings was the fact I got off the clock for the rest of the day—but only so I could scurry to class, then rush home to pass out for a few hours before another shift at work.

"Better thanks to you." He stood and handed me one of the coffees.

The height difference between us? Yeah. I loved that he towered over me, how easily he would be able to wrap me up and keep me safe...

Nope.

Reining my mind back in, I stared at the gift he offered me for a moment, knowing full well he wasn't there simply to thank me for helping him pick out cold medication. His eyes had held interest even though I wasn't his usual...cup of tea.

And oh, the temptation. The draw between us was cliché, like magnets, but no better simile existed.

I wanted to plaster myself against him, close my eyes, and sink clear through his skin until I didn't have to think anymore.

Sighing at the fact I didn't have time or trust for those things with anyone, I decided to at least not be rude and dismissive. Besides, who would turn down a free cup of Dunks?

Our fingers brushed as I took the cup, and same as at the store, a shot of something yummy swirled its way straight to my core and made me need to squeeze my thighs together.

"Thanks." I took a sip, my attention on his smiling face as the right hint of sweetness hit my tongue. "Mmm." I couldn't help my body's natural reaction to the warmth sliding down my throat.

"Two sugars, one cream," he said with a cocky smirk.

"How'd you know?"

He shrugged with nonchalance even though his eyes glinted with arrogance that I didn't find attractive. At all.

Okay, so maybe I did just a tiny bit.

"Just seemed right," he murmured, his tone lowered as he stepped a bit closer.

"Well done." I offered a forced, fake-as-hell smile as my pulse skyrocketed into outer space.

His grin widened as though not getting my standoffish vibe, but at least he stuck his free hand in his pocket rather than attempting to touch me.

I refused to drop my gaze to check out the bulge his movement drew attention to.

Nope. Not looking. Not thinking about those hands on me either.

"So?" I raised a brow and waited for him to get to his point so I could turn him down flat and erase that upward curl lingering on his luscious looking lips.

"I'd love to take you out to dinner this weekend."

My insides purred at being pursued by such a beautiful man.

"Thanks, but no." I shifted my purse forward, hinting I

wanted to get up the stairs and away from the temptation of him.

He blinked as though baffled. "Why not?"

I tilted my head to the side, loving how he seemed off kilter—and that of all people *I* had been the one to make him that way. "You're not used to hearing the word no, are you?"

His grin returned. "Can't say that I am."

"Well, Mr. Harper, I'll be honest—I know who you are and what you're like."

"And what's that?" he asked, his tone teasing.

I took a sip of my coffee, enjoying our exchange entirely too damn much. "Unlike this perfect cup of coffee, you're not my type."

He laughed, and tingles simmered low in my belly. "What's *not your type*?"

"A playboy who's well aware of how hot he is and has a different woman every night of the week."

His smirk dissolved as though I'd cut his knees out from beneath him. "That's quite a conclusion for having just met me."

"Please." I rolled my eyes even though the tiniest bit of guilt slithered through my mind over his response. "Have you *seen* your social media? It screams cocky with a hint of arrogance liberally sprinkled with blonde bimbo bling. You're wasting your time trying to get into my panties, Mr. Harper."

He stepped closer, peering down at me as though attempting to talk me onto his dick with those heated eyes and the slow smile of his lips. And that damn dimple. "So what you're saying is you've been checking me out online."

Ugh.

No point in trying to backtrack. I'd definitely set myself up for that one.

"I will not be the next notch on your bedpost," I stated, my chin lifting as a ripple of lust slid down my spine and pebbled my skin beneath his steady gaze.

He loomed over me, but I didn't back down even though the muggy heat seemed to press us closer together. He seemed the type of man to chase after prey.

But in the good way—like slamming my back up against a wall and devouring me whole.

Yum.

Shivers slid down my spine, and I fought the need to visibly gulp and give away exactly how he made me feel.

"I think you need to loosen up, little birdie," he finally said with a knowing smile and an assured tone.

I huffed a snort at his nickname. "No."

His eyes twinkled like stars at midnight, the kind you wished upon while hoping they would make your dreams come true. "I'm not above begging."

I swallowed hard, my heartbeat thumping at the image in my head of him dropping to his knees and pleading for a taste of the arousal between my thighs.

"You know you want to," he said, his gaze roaming down to the pulse jumping in my neck and the furled points of my nipples straining against my shirt.

Clutching my purse to my chest, I sidestepped to escape him before I caved to his charms. "I have to go," I attempted to sound firm, hurrying up the stairs on shaking legs.

"See you tomorrow, little birdie," I heard him call as I unlocked my apartment door and fought to force it open in the damp heat.

Damn, damn, damn.

Eyes closed, I shut myself in the cool air-conditioned

apartment and leaned back against the door. A measure of relief relaxed my shoulders—I'd held strong in denying him —but part of me had hoped he *would* get on his knees and beg.

Or chase...

Little brown-haired, white-trash Wren going out to dinner with a man like Blake Harper?

I snorted and tossed my bag onto the table.

"No way in hell," I spoke my mind, but my body argued, arousal slick inside my panties and leaving me breathless.

Shower time—and I had a date with my trusty vibrator who wouldn't ever let me down. It could also be recharged whenever needed and wouldn't ever walk away with my heart.

The perfect boyfriend if only the damn thing had arms to hold me. Caress me.

I might have imagined Blake touching me while edging myself to the point of earth-shattering bliss beneath the hot spray.

I definitely bit my tongue to keep from gasping his name as I came.

Chapter 4

Blake

Those meds Wren had suggested ended up working like a damn charm. I could smell her sweetness—berries—and had sucked her scent deep into my lungs as she'd stared up at me with stubborn fire in her eyes that made my dick hard.

She'd feigned disinterest, pretended I didn't turn her on, but her body didn't lie as easily as her lips. Her pulse had thumped in her neck as I'd stepped in close. And those perky nipples of hers had begged for my fingers and teeth to play with them until she moaned and arched into my touch.

I'd never felt such a power trip, and I wanted more of that shit. Craved it.

"Well?" Reid asked as I walked into the trailer office and adjusted my junk she'd kicked into full-on fuck mode.

"Says I'm not her type," I muttered to my best friend and foreman, my brow furrowed as I rounded the folding metal chair he sprawled in.

Reid barked with laughter, propping his feet up on my desk as I collapsed into my seat with my legs spread wide to ease the tight confines of my pants.

"She has you figured out already, huh?"

"Yeah," I muttered the truth, my usual confidence rocked from her turning me down.

One scroll through my social media had revealed my lifestyle, but the fact I tended toward extravagance in all things hadn't ever disgusted a woman before. Most salivated over the chance to spend my money and sit on my dick.

I didn't mind being seen as a beautiful face and a sure good time because it meant getting laid whenever the fuck I wanted, but I'd never felt so judged.

I fucking *hated* the churn in my stomach, the memory of the assuming expression on Wren's face. My past hadn't ever bothered me before, but her words had made me feel... soiled in some way. As though I wasn't good enough for her.

My brow furrowed deeper.

"Sucks for you."

"No shit." I glanced out the window at the old Victorian house across the street, imagining Wren climbing into the shower and sudsing up all her soft curves...or straight lines. Fuck, I still didn't have a hint of what she looked like under those clothes, but my body didn't care one way or the other.

I wanted the woman with a deep-seated need I couldn't name. There was just something about her, an intrinsic hold on my focus that demanded my attention...

"Earth to Blake."

"Fuck off," I muttered, turning back toward my best friend and shoving thoughts of a naked Wren from my head. "I need a taste of that sweet little woman, then I'll be fine and back to normal."

He barked a laugh, his dark eyes full of mirth.

"I'm serious!" I insisted with a tone that sounded like I would die without her or some such shit.

"She's got you by the short curlies already, huh?"

I snorted. "I keep that shit trimmed for a reason, asshole."

But if she wanted to tug on them, I wouldn't stop her. It was like a single connection of our eyes had captured me. One intimate touch from her and I would be all done.

That should have scared the shit out of me but didn't. I kind of...enjoyed the shiver down my spine.

"Better wax or shave then," Reid said, "because I've never seen you this way before."

My best friend knew no woman had ever caught my attention like a mouse in a trap. Even without a smile, Wren had snagged me.

That moment would haunt me until I got what I wanted so I could walk away.

"I can change her mind," I stated, knowing from past experience how easily women caved to being my sole focus. "She won't be able to resist me if I turn on the charm."

"You're such an arrogant asshole."

"Shut the fuck up," I muttered, searching my cluttered desk for something to throw at his head. All I came up with was a pencil, which flew from my grasp.

He batted it from the air with a backward swat and leaned down to pick up the projectile that had landed on the floor without causing him any damage. "Just speaking the truth," he reasoned with a grin and tossed the pencil back onto my desk.

He did. Always had with me. It was one of the things I appreciated most about Reid. He'd never once cared about the old money my mom had come from or her maiden name that sometimes put my face on the news.

I was a senator's grandson who enjoyed life to the fullest, but at least I'd inherited my father's work ethic and didn't just blow through my trust fund like my younger sister had done. She'd ended up having to move with my snow bird parents to Florida the fall before.

Putting in the hours to add to my bank account had never been a problem for me. Besides, I loved getting my hands dirty and sweating alongside my employees. I never shied away from hard work—or a challenge.

Not that I'd had any issues picking up women before though.

But with Wren? The idea of changing her aversion to me riled my thoughts toward pursue and conquer. Made me want to rub my hands together like some evil villain.

"What's on your mind, Harper?" Reid asked.

"She'd be worth the effort, no fucking doubt," I mused, ready to strip down her hesitancy and leave her sated and smiling beneath me. "It'll take weeks for me to fulfill all my fantasies about that woman that have sprung to life in the past two hours."

Reid didn't respond, and I turned my attention back to him to find his eyes widened and eyebrows raised.

"What?" I asked.

He shook his head. "In all the years I've known your fickle ass, you've never said anything like that."

"Like what?"

"Wanting more than your usual one-and-done, next, please."

"One girl got her claws into me," I countered, hating to even bring her up.

"Goddamn spoiled brat." Reid huffed with a snicker. "That was high school, man. Let it go."

I couldn't even after all those years. The mocking laughter I'd been met with...

I'd never told Reid the truth of why she'd broken my

heart, because even he didn't know about that part of me I kept hidden from everyone but my parents and my sister.

"Sure this is what you want?" Reid asked when I didn't respond. "Can't have a woman getting all clingy and trying to tie you down."

I shrugged at his reminder of what I'd always said and chugged my lukewarm coffee. I'd had plenty of those types in my past. We both had, especially the ones out to fulfill their fantasies of having two guys at the same time. Reid and I knew how to please a woman alone, but together? We blasted them to the stars, gave them memories to last a lifetime.

Reid huffed an amused snort while sprawling even deeper into the chair on the other side of my desk. "You don't even know the girl, and you're already wrapped around her little finger."

The fuck I was.

I just had plans and saw her clear as hell in my mind. She could cling to my body, and I wouldn't even be aware she was there. Small—but far from fragile if the confidence in her tilted chin and the sass in her eyes gave any indication of her real personality.

"I'd rather she have her lips wrapped around my cock." I went with my usual crude, selfish assholery the world expected of me since I'd worn the skin for so damn long it came naturally.

"And what if she's not into sucking dick?"

"Then I'll eat her pussy until she comes all over my face."

"Fuck." Reid shifted on his seat.

"Good flashback?" I asked with a grin, remembering for myself the woman we'd shared the weekend before.

"What was her name?" he asked.

"Robyn."

"Yeah." His voice rumbled. "Robyn. She was delicious. Even I was tempted to ask for seconds."

I honestly couldn't remember much more than she'd tasted like sweet cream, and I had no wish to think on that hookup any longer. My mind had been warped like light speed thanks to the little birdie, changing my course, my vision.

Wren wanted me regardless of her thoughts toward me. Her body didn't lie. I just had to find a way to make her desire trump her brain.

Since Wren had really stalked me online like it sounded she'd done, I definitely had my work cut out for me in getting her stripped down to satisfy my lust so I could move on.

At least I wouldn't have to worry about her trying to put permanent relationship shackles on me like dozens of others had in the past.

Maybe her lack of interest in my money was what had drawn me to her...

Getting emotionally pulled into that kind of woman would be as hopeless as Picard resisting the Borg.

But I could do it.

No woman would ever assimilate me into the "norm" like my parents had hopes of for me considering our family name. I would never adapt what I enjoyed in order to fulfill others' dreams and plans for my future. My life was my own to live as I saw fit.

Resistance *wouldn't* be futile.

I pushed away my thoughts and the inner nerd I never let out to play anymore. That shit stayed buried deep as fuck beneath the armored exterior I wore.

I had to have Wren Shipman, and that was the end of it.

Once I had the weak spot she'd created inside me figured out, I would strike hot and hard.

Pulling out my cell, I began a search for Wren. Two social media sites had private accounts with nothing more than a picture of her in profile, showing that slight cleft in her chin.

Cute as fuck, I mused, unable to help my smile over the memory of the sass and fire she portrayed for someone so small.

"Oh my God, Blake," Reid's snorted words lifted my focus off my cell. "Fucking heart eyes? Really?"

"Nah." I flashed him a grin that didn't feel at all genuine. "Like you said, she's got me by the short and curlies. Now, if I can just get her grip elsewhere—"

"On your dick or heart?" Reid asked.

"—so I can get her *out of my head.*" I emphasized the rest of my thought after his rudeness.

His humor evaporated as he studied me. "I'm having sudden visions of no more sharing women, and that fucking sucks. She's seriously got you all tied up."

"Far from it," I waved him off even though that tingle of nameless something made me want to shift in my chair.

My heart wasn't available for the taking, but I would gladly put my body at her disposal.

Like all women, she would eventually see the worth of being on my arm. Once she realized what a good time I could be, she would cave and give me what I wanted.

One night. Maybe two.

Then I could get back to the life as a playboy who was content, thank you *very* much.

An idea popped into my head, one sure way to sway her into bed if she fantasized like a lot of women did. I ignored the first-time-ever twisting in my stomach over the thought of sharing a woman.

"Would you be up for a threesome if she's game?" I asked, casting a glance over at my best friend.

His slow smirk was answer enough.

Chapter 5

Wren

Tuesday morning, and I got home to once more find Blake sitting on my bottom step. He held a Dunks and bakery bag in his hands.

Inside my head, I growled, hating how my exhausted body perked right up at the sight of him.

His grin didn't send a twinge of need through my core, nor did the slide of his dark blue eyes over my rumpled uniform.

Nope.

A definite no.

Lies.

"What do you want?" I snipped, keeping a few feet of distance between us so my body didn't betray the truth taunting my brain.

He took his time standing, stretching out those long legs and making me have to tilt my head back to keep my focus on his gorgeous face.

A natural swoon rose up inside me that I had to choke off with a hard swallow.

"Good morning to you too," he said with a smirk, those

damn eyes of his twinkling as though he knew exactly what his presence did to me regardless of my mindset to not sway toward him.

"I beg to differ," I sniffed, lifting my chin.

"This'll help." He handed over the coffee and bag, but I simply raised an eyebrow and pretended my large duffel was already too much for me to handle.

"I can bring these upstairs for you," he offered with a smirk while lifting the gifts he'd bought for me.

Snorting, I slung my duffel over my head because I wasn't about to pass up a snack and a hot coffee. And I sure as hell wasn't about to let him step foot into my personal safe place where all my walls would come tumbling down.

Ignoring the fact I had a pot brewed in my small kitchen, I took his offering. "If you expect to get anything in return for these," I muttered, lifting the cup to my lips, "you're wasting your time."

"Hmm," he hummed, watching closely as I swigged and swallowed. "*I beg to differ*," he tossed back, using my own words against me.

I tried not to grin. "You aren't my type," I reminded him, hating that he just somehow knew how I loved my coffee.

He shoved his hands into his pockets.

Once again, I refused to check out the bulge they bracketed.

"So you said—but you haven't even given me a chance, Wren."

Offer him the opportunity to prove he wasn't a playboy? That his social media was just smoke and mirrors hiding a delicious cinnamon soul beneath his gorgeous exterior? Someone who could be loving and loyal to the lucky woman who captured his heart?

Yeah right.

I lifted an eyebrow but was too damn curious to hear what he had to say before shutting him down with a snipped reply.

"You seem the sort that works too hard and never plays," he murmured when I didn't comment.

He wasn't wrong, but I took another mouthful of hot deliciousness rather than admitting to my pathetic existence. There was a reason I chose to live the way I did. Not that a wealthy man like him would ever understand.

"You need a night out," he said, glancing over my rumpled work clothes. "Dinner. Maybe dancing."

He sounded just like any other guy who'd ever hit on me.

Nothing new.

Just another damn notch.

"And let me guess," I said, my voice dry, "you think you're the perfect man to give me that."

His slow smirk brought all sorts of lively activity to life between my thighs when I should have rolled my eyes.

I scowled.

"You need to let loose, little birdie," he said, leaning toward me the slightest bit and sending a shockwave through every cell in my body. "Be excessive for a change. Live a little."

Although he spoke truth, I bristled over his limited perception and arrogance. He had no clue where I'd come from. My lack of the barest essentials he'd probably taken for granted every day of his childhood.

"Funny we met less than twenty-four hours ago and you think you know what's best for me," I stated firmly. "Honestly, Blake, I was serious when I said you aren't my type.

The last guy I need in my life right now is some selfish asshole who's only interested in one thing."

"Ouch," he breathed with a grimace. "You've got me all wrong, baby—"

I snorted. "Don't call me baby."

"Don't presume to know me," he shot back, the traces of teasing and flirting gone from his face. "You have no idea who I truly am, the shit I've had to deal with."

One of my eyebrows arched, and I wished I could cross my loaded down arms. "Senator's grandson, tons of money... what sort of *shit* is having life handed to you on a silver spoon?"

A muscle ticked in his jaw, but it was well past time to end his pursuit. The sooner the guy learned I wasn't on the smorgasbord he had a habit of gorging on, the sooner we could both get back to our lives.

"You're judging me again," he stated quietly, his gaze flitting over my face as though looking for a crack to weasel his way through.

My chin lifted. "I'm not interested in doing anything else with you."

He actually flinched. "Harsh."

I pressed my lips tight, refusing to pull any punches.

"I promise you'll have a good time." The arrogant bastard pushed even though my blunt honesty would have pissed most men off and sent them stalking away.

"Not going to happen."

"I'm persistent." He eyes did the twinkle thing again that did *not* flutter my belly.

I narrowed my gaze while glaring up at him, heat in my cheeks. Our exchange should have pissed me off, not left me...achy and empty for stuff I couldn't yet afford in my life. "And I'm stubborn."

One side of his mouth curled upward, causing butter-flies to erupt in my belly. "I kinda noticed. Think it's sexy as hell too."

Goddamn this man to hell and back again.

He knew how to talk the talk, that was for damned sure. Butter her up. Rain compliments down over her thirsty ears. As long as he kept those big hands to himself...

A shiver slid over my skin.

"You're not going to get what you want this time around," I stated firmly although my body begged me just give in already.

"What if it's what *you* want?" he asked, but before I could lie again, he continued. "Every woman has fantasies, right? Especially that threesome with two men who both give her their undivided attention."

Yeah, he got me there, but I wasn't about to admit to that either.

"How about I take you out, and we bring my best friend Reid along as a...buffer. Third wheel kinda thing. It's what he does best."

"Who the hell is he, and why would I agree to that when *I'm not interested in you*?"

Blake's gaze slid down my neck and lingered on the hardened tips of my breasts I couldn't hide. "You are, but for some strange reason you just don't want to admit it."

"I don't do playboys," I muttered, hating how every inch of my body except for my brain ignored all the red flags waving around Blake. "Thanks for breakfast, but I have class in an hour." I slid past him and started up the stairs.

"Class?"

"Not everyone has shit handed to them," I called over my shoulder, snark obvious as hell in my tone.

"What are you taking classes for?"

I continued stomping as I climbed the stairs. Why the hell did he push—or even care for that matter? Reaching the landing, I turned and looked down on the guy I'd been too caught up in the previous couple of weeks.

"I'm going to school to be a pharmacist so I can get the stench of my childhood off me." The truth spilled without thought, and my lips went tight as heat rushed to my face.

He stared up at me for a few seconds as though trying to figure out the meaning of my too-honest answer. "That's what? Six, seven years?" he finally asked.

"Six."

His smile made him look like a sweet boy next door, his usual cockiness completely absent.

Although my shoulders relaxed, I didn't trust the interest he seemed to show in my life outside getting me under him.

"How long until you're finished?" he asked.

"Next spring."

"Impressive. Gotta be expensive as hell though."

For someone like you, my mind tacked on the words I expected he'd swallowed down considering my car and the ramshackle house I lived in.

My chin lifted again, and I slowly perused his perfect form from head to toe. It was time to let him know where I stood and why. Maybe he'd get the freaking hint.

"I'm making something of myself, *by* myself, and I'm going to finish without useless distraction." There. Firmly stated without any possibility of being swayed off my course.

Blake studied me, and I held still, hoping he got that little jab I'd intended for extra oomph.

Not everyone got shit handed to them.

His slow smirk and that damn dimple popping out did

not shoot a little adrenaline into my blood stream. "Need any help studying?"

I held his stare even though I would have rather gone soft like putty, pliant and willing to be formed into whatever made him happy. "Goodbye, Blake Harper."

"See ya around, Wren Shipman."

Goddamn the man and his lively eyes that promised he wasn't anywhere near done trying to get me to bend to his wishes.

Growling under my breath, I shoved into my apartment door and locked up behind me, pissed off that I wasn't truly angry. His stubbornly pursuing me shouldn't have intrigued me. Shouldn't have made that magnetic pull ten times stronger. Shouldn't have intensified the arousal between my thighs for a little of whatever he packed between his.

I didn't drop my shit on the table and hug the window to watch him stroll across the street as though he didn't have a care in the world.

I didn't drool over his flexing thighs and rounded backside that made me think about biting into a crunchy apple.

And I didn't jerk back from view when he lifted his head and looked my way before going into his trailer office.

Big. Fat. Lies. I'd done all three with my heart in my throat and a war in my head.

His second attempt at getting into my pants had proven just as fruitless as the first, but a part of me craved to let my reserve crumble to dust and just give in to whatever the hell pull he'd created. A sort of...undeniable attraction that had connected us by some life-giving force.

He'd all but promised a threesome, a definite bucket list item of mine, but tempting as it was, I could *not* chance a quick fuck with someone like him. Blake was too...potent in every way. One caress, one feel of those strong arms around me, and I would fall for a guy who would take off as fast as my father had left Mom.

Turning my chair away from the window, I sat and enjoyed the blueberry muffin he'd bought for me. A sweet gift made even better by the perfect cup of coffee.

But he couldn't buy himself a space between my thighs.

Or behind me.

Or get me on my knees.

Or even held up against a wall.

Gulping at the sudden rush of slickness on my panties, I shook my head.

Pulling my notebook for that morning's class across the table from where I'd left my homework the night before, I focused my brain on what was important.

That definitely didn't include Blake Harper, his luscious body, or whoever the hell Reid might be.

His sexy foreman?

"Oh shit." I thumped my forehead onto the kitchen table and let out a heavy exhale. "Get your thoughts back in line, Wren," I grumbled to myself, lifting my gaze once more. "You've got more important stuff to think about."

Color coded precise notes lined the papers in front of me, but not one word made sense as I attempted to study for that morning's quiz.

Chapter 6

Blake

I'd gotten under Wren's skin but not in the way I'd hoped for. True annoyance had lined her face regardless of how I turned her body on.

Rather than pester the woman day after day until she relented, I decided to pull back a bit and regroup. Reevaluate my plan to conquer her because she was just...Christ, I couldn't even figure out how the hell she made me feel.

I just needed to touch her skin. Taste her mouth. Have her perfect little body wrapped up in mine.

But I had no fucking game since I'd never been so properly set aside in my life. She didn't want the front every other woman did, so how could I get inside her head in order to get her out of mine?

Friday night, I went out with Reid and a couple of guys I'd been friends with since high school. Reid scoped the place out like he always did, deciding which woman's night he would make. Colton was also one of my employees and milked his first beer with slumped shoulders.

Micah lounged at the high top table across from me, scanning the lively bar around us with eyes like a summer sky. His blond hair tended toward mussed like mine—and also like me, he rarely had issues picking up women.

But he enjoyed...*more* with his hookups and not in the way of feelings.

While I was all about gently marking up skin with my fingers and mouth, he tended toward floggers and that sort of shit.

To each his own though.

Micah also owned Elite Escorts, a high-end booty call business that promised satisfaction with a money-back guarantee. He'd done quite well for himself too. Earlier that morning, he'd stopped by the jobsite to drop off some plans for his office remodel and had mentioned needing to hire a couple more guys. He'd been all over both Reid and Colton to join his team for months.

Micah glanced over at Colton whose shoulders slouched as he checked his cell. "What's up with you?"

Colton tucked away his phone and went back to toying with his half-empty bottle that had to be warm as fuck. "Sorry."

"You look like someone stole your puppy."

I snorted, damn near spewing a mouthful of beer across the table. Even if the guy seriously did appear that way, Micah hadn't come anywhere near the mark of what bugged our friend.

"He's pining over a married couple," Reid answered before I could explain my reaction or Colton's pouting. "A daddy and mommy he can call his own."

Oh shit. I glanced between the two men.

"You're lucky I like you, Sullivan, or I would pound you to shit," Colton shot at Reid, fire in his dark eyes.

Reid chuckled and sipped his beer while I raised an eyebrow, waiting for things to go south.

Colton had grown up in foster care, so Reid's word choices hadn't been the smartest—but we always busted Colton's chops about the silver fox whose hands he wanted on him and the curvy wife who rounded out our friend's idea of heaven.

"What happened?" Micah asked, giving Colton his full attention once it became apparent Colton had no intention of flattening Reid's nose like I'd expected. Colton tended to lose his shit sometimes...or at least, he used to when he was younger. It seemed age had chilled him the fuck out a bit.

Colton filled Micah in on the couple Reid and I had already learned about a few weeks earlier.

Colton had built a deck for the Youngs who'd hired Harper's Construction, and he'd gotten his panties in a twist over the both of them. Things for him had turned even worse when the Youngs had invited our friend over for a night of poly playtime.

But Colton wanted more and had gotten his little heart broken when that silver fox sent him packing after their one-and-done sex fest.

Poor sap. That was what happened when you went looking for love in hookups. But, if the man wanted it...

"Still think you need to try again," I said about his giving up so easily and sipped my beer.

"No means no." Micah shot out before Colton could reply.

"That's why I'm sitting here with your sorry asses and not over at their house begging for another chance," Colton muttered, peeling at his beer bottle's label.

Micah pulled his buzzing cell from his back pocket, swiped the screen to life, and frowned. "Fuck." His fingers flew while texting. He stopped and waited, his focus on the screen. "One of my guys is puking his guts up and had to cancel tonight. Goddamnit." He started texting again, groaned, and scanned around our small table, his gaze landing on each of us one at time as though sizing up which of us he could talk into being an Elite fill-in.

"No. Nope." Reid drank down the rest of his beer. "I've got plans."

"What plans?" Micah asked.

"See that little blonde over there?" Reid motioned with his head toward the bar while sliding off his stool. "She's an old hookup from a few weeks ago and has been giving me eyes all night. I'll see you losers later."

"Asshole!" I called after him. He was supposed to pay for the next round.

Reid flicked me off over his shoulder.

"Colton?" Micah asked. "All you gotta do is sit and watch. It's a married couple who are newly into exploring their kinky sides which is pretty much just exhibition but in the privacy of their own home. Less than an hour—I'll give you two hundred cash."

"Sorry, no can do," Colton muttered.

"Blake—"

"No fucking way." I shook my head. It was the first time he'd ever asked me, but I had a too well-known face to be posing as an escort. And I didn't need any help getting laid.

Actually...I did with the one I had yet to entice into bed, but Wren definitely didn't seem the sort who would pay for a fuck.

"Come on! I'm desperate over here!"

"I'm stuck on this little birdie who lives across the street from the condo project," I said, "and she's everything I've ever wanted."

Well, for a night or two, anyway. Just until I got her out from beneath my skin.

Why did that thought feel like a lie?

I shifted on my chair, clearing my throat.

"All you gotta do is watch," Micah said, leaning forward to prop his elbows on the table, those blue eyes of his intense as fuck. I wouldn't submit to his dominance though. The fucker had to know that by now.

I grinned.

"No touch, no taste, no nothing but keeping your eyes open and enjoy the show," he pushed with a tone that refused argument, but I wasn't turned on by that power dynamic shit like the little subbies he played with.

"Thought you said no means no?"

Micah snorted while sitting back in his chair again, muscular arms crossing and stretching his T-shirt tight over his shoulders. "This isn't the same thing, and you know it."

We went back and forth a bit, and I had fun with our banter while watching Micah grow antsy and agitated, something he rarely portrayed in his constant need for control.

"Please, Blake," he finally broke, pleading lacing his voice. "I'm fucking begging. I'll owe you one."

I narrowed my gaze, studying my friend who hated to be beholden to any man. Seriously, what could it hurt to just sit and watch a married couple go at it? I might even enjoy it a bit like any other time I saw and watched people hook up. Maybe learn a thing or two—nope. Doubtful. Two people who'd been together for a long time...they'd probably requested an escort to watch them fuck in order to bring some excitement into their relationship again.

Okay, so I wouldn't learn jack shit, but who wouldn't get off on a little live porn?

It wasn't like I had plans outside sitting there and drinking a couple more beers. I wasn't about to try to pick up a woman since all I could think about was that tiny birdie who smelled like berries and seemed too damn perfect for my own good.

"You'll owe me two," I suggested, shoving aside thoughts of what I couldn't figure out how to get.

"Deal." Micah stuck out his hand across the table without further haggling.

"You might regret this," I warned, clasping his hand and settling my plans for the rest of the night into concrete.

He offered to call me an Uber, but I assured him I'd only had two beers in two hours and wasn't even buzzed.

A few minutes after I climbed into my car, a text came through with an address for one of the luxury condos down on Beacon Hill.

Micah: **I appreciate this.**

Chuckling, I texted him back. **Just don't get any ideas about adding me to your payroll on any regular schedule.**

Micah: **Your love of watching isn't a secret.**

Yeah, Micah, Reid, and Colton all knew that firsthand, and we'd shared all sorts of shit on guys' Friday nights out.

Micah: **This couple are regular clients. They get off on having someone shifting in the shadows and moaning along while they fuck.**

I frowned, suddenly a little apprehensive about the whole affair. **You didn't say anything about my having to put on a vocal show. And I'm not going to get off seeing some old couple go at it.**

Micah: **They aren't old. And I've seen them live. Good luck not busting a nut in your drawers.**

I snorted a laugh and tucked my cell away before

pulling out of the parking lot. While I *was* a bit of a voyeur at heart, I wasn't about to whip out my dick and enjoy earning that two-hundred bucks Micah had promised me any more than I had to.

11

Wrong.

Fuck, had I been wrong.

Mrs. Renshaw looked just like Wren minus the glasses. As for her body, the mid-thirties woman had more straight lines than curves, but her confidence...

What a gorgeous sight she was riding her husband's dick, long hair hanging down her back, ass jiggling with every upward slam of Mr. Renshaw's hips. She was a moaner too. All, *give me more, harder,* and *love your thick cock so damn much, baby.*

Lounged back in an embroidered chair in the shadows just like Micah had said, I kept shifting to relieve the tightness of my jeans. Hands fisted on my thighs, I glanced at the box of tissues, lube, and wipes on the small table beside me.

Such gracious hosts with those kind gifts while the view a mere fifteen feet in front of me was downright mean in the best way possible.

I'd always loved watching, but something about the way the woman moved made my blood fucking burn. Her body gyrating in a fluid motion like a belly dancer...hips all sensual swaying, hands feeling up her curves and into her hair.

Pure sex. Absolute lust.

The Renshaws needed to start an OnlyFans account and broadcast their chemistry to heat up cooler-blooded couples. Hell, I'd have paid good money to watch them rather than cheesy porn sites. Their connection was downright palatable. I could taste their love, their dedication, in the thick air. Could smell their want and hear the sounds of their fucking...no lube, just pure creamy pussy and pre-cum making a smeared mess between their bodies.

Fuuuck.

I rubbed a hand over my face, my entire body tensed and ready to bust that nut Micah had prophesied.

They had me so damn close...and they still went at it like rabbits.

The mister tossed his wife onto her back and dove into her pussy like a starved man, and I couldn't help my responding groan as he made his vocal appreciation of her taste.

No man had ever turned me on, but Mr. Renshaw's literal growl over her cream on his tongue?

Fuck yeah.

My balls tightened, and knowing I couldn't just get up and walk out until they finished, I realized I had to relieve some pressure.

They wouldn't mind, so why should I?

If I'd been watching them on a screen from the privacy of my own home, I'd have had my cock in hand a half hour earlier.

A pop of my button, a slide of my zipper, and I hissed in relief at the space I allowed my aching dick. But that wasn't enough. I eased my hand into my boxer briefs and pulled my length upright, completely free from its prison.

Pre-cum beaded on my slit, but I reached for that pump bottle of lube.

Perfect. I bit back a groan while smearing that slick shit up and down my entire length.

Mr. Renshaw slid upward between his wife's splayed thighs, his tongue dragging over her taut belly and tits before shoving into her mouth at the same time he thrust into her core.

I bit into my lower lip, seeing Wren beneath me.

Writhing.

Moaning.

Begging for more.

Her fingernails digging into my spine, heels clutching at my ass as I pounded into her over and over again, taking her apart with my cock.

I wanted her whimpers in my ears, her lips parted on gasps against mine. Wanted her sweat on my skin and her tight core clutching at my girth like a vise.

Squeezing the base of my dick, I fought to keep from unloading.

Fucking stamina...Mr. Renshaw behaved like a beast, wrecking his tiny wife—but she only pleaded for more. Begged him to love her harder. Take her apart and put her back together again like only he could.

He wrapped his hand around her neck, cutting off her oxygen, and licked between her parted lips as she gasped for breath.

That did it. I fucking lost it.

Yanking my shirt up high, I tucked it between my teeth and jerked the hell out of my cock, lewd schlicking noises as loud as their fucking. Nostrils flared, I sucked air into my lungs.

A lone curse tore from my lips at the first spurt of cum up over my abs, and I grunted with the next three, my focus still ensnared by the writhing woman.

"Fuck," I huffed a half-mutter as one last tremor ripped through me—and Mrs. Renshaw shrieked her release as though finally giving in since they had satisfied my watchful eyes.

My skin pebbled as I sank back into the chair, muscles lax, while they finished together as though their minds moved in sync.

I'd never, not *once*, climaxed at the same time as whoever lay on the receiving end of my cock.

Their eyes remained locked, their emotions once more making themselves known in how they kissed and petted each other, their soft words of love barely reaching my ears. A slight ache spread over my chest, and I rubbed at it absently, allowing myself to wonder what it felt like to have a deep connection beyond the physical.

To want so much that all you could see was them.

To love so damn hard that your life existed in another's gaze.

To feel the type of feelings that bonded souls together regardless of differences.

Swallowing hard, I grabbed a wad of tissues and cleaned myself before tucking my spent dick away.

By the time I finished wiping up, Mr. Renshaw had pulled out from his wife's body and sat back on his haunches.

"Okay, my sweet?" he asked, soothing palms down the insides of her splayed thighs.

"Better than," she murmured, her face flushed and her eyes full of love while she gazed at him.

I want that—

Fuck no I didn't. No woman would ever accept the closet nerd beneath my outward appearance. The man who had insecurities just like every other guy regardless of money, prestige, or the show he put on for the world to see.

Mr. Renshaw leaned down and pressed his lips to hers. "I'll see him out then draw us a bath."

My cue to leave.

I tossed the tissues into the small trash can beside the chair and stood, my legs a little unstable. It had been months since I'd felt that kind of release...maybe years. Hell, I wasn't sure I remembered a full body experience where every sense got wrapped up in—

Wren.

Stomach bottoming out along with my crashed lungs, I blinked. *What* had she done to me?

Completely uncaring of his nudity, Mr. Renshaw approached, his steps bringing him into the shadows where I'd sat and fixing me firmly once more in the present.

"She enjoyed having you here," he said with a half-cocked smile.

One of my eyebrows shot up. His wife hadn't even looked at me, but considering how close the Renshaws appeared to be, I wouldn't have been surprised to learn he could read her mind.

"My pleasure," I said, my voice nothing more than sand and gravel.

He flashed a grin and motioned toward their bedroom door.

I led the way, and he followed on my heels until I reached the entryway where he'd greeted me a couple hours earlier.

"We hope to see you again, Blake." Mr. Renshaw didn't offer his hand, and I was fine with not having to touch the dried pussy juice and cum he smelled of.

"Give Micah a holler," I heard myself suggest, realizing as I said it I wouldn't turn down another chance to enjoy him and his wife get their exhibition kink on.

A text awaited me when I hopped in my car.

Micah: **You're welcome.**

I barked a laugh and let him know he'd been right, that his customers were the hottest live porn show I'd seen to date.

Micah: **So does this mean I can book you next time they call?**

I didn't even hesitate before answering since watching Mrs. Renshaw would have to pacify my wants for Wren until I could get her out of my damn head.

Chapter 7

Wren

Blake surprised me. His persistent ass didn't sit on my bottom step waiting for me to get home from work every morning so he could pressure me into a date like I'd expected.

But he left gifts on occasion.

Piping hot coffee and muffins. A small pot of violets. A little wren figurine that curled my lips into a smile I didn't want to give him but did with my back turned toward the jobsite. Handwritten notes of encouragement to brighten my day—and I hated that they did.

No one had ever been there for me when I really needed it, and as though Blake had somehow managed to see into my exhausted brain, he hit my feels like some boxer smashing against my walls. His short one or two-liner pep talks and inspiration to keep plugging along in attaining my goals boosted me on more mornings than I wished to count.

I tucked those folded pieces of paper away in my bedside table drawer, refusing to cherish them in my mind as much as I couldn't help but do in my heart.

Not once did I glance over my shoulder to see if he watched me pick up those precious gifts.

Not once did I traipse across the street to thank him since he would see the tears in my eyes his kind words had prompted.

And not once did I admit out loud that my heart had softened toward the cocky guy who I'd begun to think wasn't really an asshole.

I took all those gifts and treasured them in my third-floor apartment that had officially lost its view of the river. But I couldn't blame the gorgeous man for that. He'd merely been hired to erect the building to give the richer folks what I no longer had.

Three weeks had dragged by, and I cursed myself for having decided to tackle summer classes so I could still have time to work over the fall and winter months while taking a full load in college my final year.

I'd already gotten five years in, and although my dedication hadn't waned, my energy had about reached its end.

A phone call came in the middle of the night while I was at work that damn near took my fortitude over a bridge.

It was Melrose-Wakefield hospital notifying me that my mom had been rushed to the ER by ambulance.

Mom had been sick on and off for a couple years, but with how she'd treated her body, she shouldn't have expected any less than a shutdown of one internal organ after another. She'd already been unbalanced and suffering from mental issues for years, all brought on by long-term use of drugs.

She tended to ignore symptoms and hadn't been to a doctor that I knew of since...forever.

I left Jenny alone at the pharmacy and traveled south, unsure of what I would find upon arrival at the hospital. It had been over a month since I'd last visited my mom, and although there wasn't much love between us, she was still my mom and had done the best she could considering her addiction.

I hated the sight of her in the bed. Pale and gaunt, she appeared as though she'd lost even more weight when she hadn't been able to afford to do so.

She looked like a damn skeleton with tissue paper-like skin stretched tight atop.

Laying in the ICU hooked to monitors, IVs, and other beeping shit, she didn't even appear alive. Were it not for the slight, slow rise and fall of her chest, I'd have thought her already gone. A sense of sadness hit me, not nearly as potent as I'd expected. If I'd had a normal, healthy relationship with her, I expected my grief would have been worse. But even still, my beaten-down body sagged beneath the emotional weight.

I sat in the chair beside her, attempting to recognize features of the woman I used to know.

She'd always been thin, but she had wasted away to nothing.

Sharp cheek bones. Eye sockets like caverns. Lanky, gray-streaked hair that probably hadn't seen a brush in days. The old track marks all over her bony arms.

I didn't check beneath the sheets tucked up under her chest to see how the rest of her body had fared during what must have been a serious health decline.

Why hadn't she called?

Why hadn't she at least let me know she'd suffered?

And why the fuck hadn't she attempted to get on Medicare?

I couldn't begin to imagine the bills racking up with every tick of the clock on the wall behind me. Would the responsibility of paying them fall onto my shoulders as her only living relative?

I went light-headed at the thought since I barely managed to scrape by myself. Add in all my student loans piling atop me, and I already carried the weight of the world.

Long hours passed while I stared with burning eyes, my mind quickly overcome by the stress of the situation.

Would it be horrible if I secretly hoped she would just pass sooner than later? The dragging out of hospital care—and hospice too if she clung to life and got discharged—would drain me and our bank accounts.

Neither she nor I had anything of value worth selling. Secondhand furniture, ratty from years of use sat in both our apartments. Same with the clothes. She had no car, and I'd gotten mine for a song and dance considering the three hundred thousand miles racked up on its odometer.

Less than ten months until school finished...if I could somehow hang on until then, I could begin to dig myself out of the bottomless pit of poverty.

Maybe.

Assuming I passed my licensure examination and landed a job. I wouldn't be picky. Day or night shift, inpatient or out, I just needed better income than working as a tech.

A doctor finally made rounds toward sunrise, and I barely managed to keep my eyelids propped open while listening to him explain Mom's issues.

Liver and kidney failure with transplants being her only source of hope...a very slim one at that.

Mom had mentioned time and again that she'd grown tired of living. I doubted she would want to prolong her misery through surgeries and difficult recoveries.

Throat tight, I listened to the alternatives, which promised what she'd seemed to be craving the past couple of years.

Without surgical intervention, which he couldn't promise would actually save Mom considering her current state, he gave her a couple weeks at the most. And I had no other choice but to care for her at home. How the fuck I would do that, I didn't know.

The doctor informed me I could apply for financial aid for hospital bills and hospice, so there was that.

I cried while stumbling on my way across the parking lot toward my car. Heavy tears and runny nose, my body caved for a solid twenty minutes once I sat inside and wallowed in my miserable circumstance before I finally got a hold on myself and could see to put the key into my car's ignition.

The ride north seemed to take hours in my dazed, exhausted state, but I found myself pulling into my assigned parking spot only a few minutes later than I usually would if I'd put in my usual hours at the pharmacy.

Glancing in the rearview mirror, I noted the construction workers meandering around and the big silver truck sitting alongside the trailer office belonging to Blake Harper.

He'd grown up in privilege, never having tasted the fear and bitterness of being dirt-poor. Wondering where your next meal would come from. How you couldn't scrounge up pennies for new shoes when your tattered ones squished the hell out of your toes. When your jeans seemed to shrink two inches overnight from your one and only growth spurt. Running out of toilet paper and having to use rags to wipe your ass—then washing them with cheap bar soap because you couldn't even afford laundry detergent.

"Shit." I swallowed hard, pulling my mind from the past.

Maybe Blake had left me another note of encouragement, one about hope...because I didn't feel as though I had much left in me and desperately needed something. Some*one* to offer my aching heart comfort.

Or maybe he was personally ready for his third attempt at getting into my panties shut down.

I finally pushed my car door open, cursed the rising humidity, and climbed out on weary legs, ready to growl in annoyance and/or burst into tears if he actually showed up to pester me into going out with him.

Chapter 8

Blake

I became the reluctant voyeur for Mr. and Mrs. Renshaw. Well, not exactly reluctant per se, just more along the lines of refusing to be called an actual employee of Micah Fox's Elite Escorts.

He didn't put me on the payroll, but four more times in the following three weeks of first watching the Renshaws get down and dirty, I sat in their chair. Dreamed of Wren. Jerked off and found release all over my chest and abs.

Why the two of them specifically requested me every time they were in an exhibition mood, I had no fucking clue. I didn't make much noise other than a grunt when climaxing, didn't interact, just sat as quiet as could be and enjoyed the fuck out of Mrs. Renshaw coming on her husband's dick.

Fuck, did I have a case of the envies.

I carried home fantasies of pleasing Wren, having her shatter beneath me, her soft, pouty mouth raining down praise on how much I pleased her. Her small hands clutching at my back and cock. Her hazel-brown eyes peering into mine without a shred of judgment or disgust.

They were all dreams.

Nothing more.

Evidence being the lack of acknowledgement for the small gifts I left her on occasion. Too often, she appeared downtrodden and weary, and although I didn't know her that well, I expected working full time and studying to become a pharmacist couldn't be easy.

She never glanced my way before retrieving the morning offerings and trudging up her stairs.

Having decided that the third time was the charm, I decided to swoop in and confront Wren. Maybe those little notes I'd labored over finding online had softened her opinion of me.

Friday morning, I sat on her bottom step with no gift but myself.

She needed a night out. To be spoiled with good food, a bottle of whatever wine she preferred, and maybe even a massage by hands itching to touch her skin. Not that she'd let me that close on a first date if I even got lucky enough for her to agree to go out with me.

But with how she'd been working her ass off and dragging herself home every morning the previous couple of weeks, I expected she might at least cave to someone paying for her dinner for a change.

Wren pulled into her parking spot, and I watched the front end of her car that I could see from where I sat, my heartbeat strangely rapid. Since when did I get fucking butterflies?

I felt as though...I wanted her to like me. To see beyond the public profile I portrayed.

Straightening from where I sat, I allowed that feeling to swirl and intensify, taking me closer to grasping a name for what it was. Far beyond attraction, that was for damned sure. Intrigued—definitely. Enamored…

Wren took forever to get out of the car, and I wondered if she'd caught sight of me on the other side of her downstairs neighbor's SUV and was stalling, thinking of how to say no yet again.

Rubbing sweaty palms down my work pants, I considered standing up to get a view of her in the driver seat because I was *dying* to see her face. Get a read on how she felt about me once and for all.

The opening of her door made me hesitate, and I forced myself to stay put rather than towering over her. Maybe it was my size she hated—maybe my looming over her was a trigger of some sort. Huge guy, small girl…maybe she'd been hurt in the past, maybe—

My thought cut off at the sight of Wren's face.

Paler than normal, she had dark circles beneath her eyes and lines that had no business being on her young skin.

Our gazes clashed, her exhaustion hitting me in the gut like a meaty fist.

The fuck had happened to her?

"Morning," I murmured, not bothering with the good part since it was obvious she wouldn't agree. "You okay?" I asked, peering up at her as she closed the distance between us.

She swallowed hard as tears filled her eyes.

Oh shit. I didn't know what to do with tears. Whenever Mom or my sister got all emotional, I took the fuck off.

"I can't do this today, Blake," she whispered, her tone as watery as her eyes.

So no asking out—point noted and understood.

"Need a hug or an ear?" I offered, strangely without intent to get physically closer.

Her smile wobbled, but it was still a curving of the lips —for me. "Neither, but thank you."

I didn't budge when she glanced at the stairs behind me though. "You're *not* okay."

She hesitated but eventually whispered, "No."

"Anything I can do to help?" Never before had I felt such need to ease someone's suffering, physically or emotionally, and damn if I didn't actually *like* how it made my chest ache.

A shake of her head accompanied a half-laugh, half-choked sob.

I clenched my fists to keep from reaching for her like instinct demanded I do.

"My mom is dying." The words spilled from her lips as though holding them in would only worsen her clear exhaustion.

What the fuck did you say to something like that? I'm sorry? Offer condolences? I'd already asked if I could help, but damn.

Wren clutched her bag to her chest, and the word vomit began regardless of the fact she'd claimed she didn't want my ear.

But I didn't see or hear her unloading on me as something annoying or disgusting. She laid out her past in clear detail, not holding back what most people would be embarrassed by.

Being raised by her mom who was a drug addict, Wren had pretty much been independent by age five. Left alone for hours, sometimes days while her mom was out falling in love and bringing home strange men. Lucky for her, none had proven to be a perv or had taken advantage of her innocence while her mom passed out high as a kite.

Electricity getting shut off when only rent money could be scrounged up.

Hitting up the local food pantries and churches in order to have food in their bellies when her mom got laid off from one of a dozen jobs she'd attempted to keep.

Wren should have been tossed into the system countless times, but somehow fate had intended her to stay with the woman who'd given birth to her.

What should have been disrespect and hatred-filled words on her lips were far from either. Wren appreciated having life given to her. Chose to believe her mom had done the best she could while being addicted to drugs and unable to think properly.

I ingested every sentence, took to heart every play of emotion on Wren's beautiful, tired face, amazed by her acceptance and unconditional love for her mom.

And my heart ached with empathy and longing I didn't understand.

While sitting at Wren Shipman's feet and listening to her spill her guts to a near stranger, I realized I wanted more than just one or two nights between her thighs. I wanted to hear more than her moans while climaxing on my dick. I wanted to see her relaxed and happy, content and peaceful.

Taken care of.

Cherished.

My throat went tight at the thought of her never having had that throughout her childhood while I'd been gifted a shit ton by both of my loving parents.

Would I ever be able to convince her I was more than a playboy who'd never bothered trying to curb his appetite for pussy? That I had depth beyond my outward appearance, beyond the persona I'd worn since learning as a teenager what my looks could get me?

I'd become addicted to attention and craved meaningful relationships outside my friends, but no woman had ever made me want to be more than just a pretty face, fat wallet, and easy fuck.

Maybe Wren would be different.

But she was in no place to consider giving me a chance. She had a loaded plate overflowing with shit, and all I could do was offer myself for whatever she needed.

I fished one of my cards from my back pocket once she sagged, silent and seemingly emptied.

"What's that for?" she whispered, wiping tear tracks from her cheeks instead of taking the card from my outstretched hand.

"The offer of my ear if you ever need it again."

She huffed a quiet laugh, shaking her head. "I just spilled all the filth of my past woes to you like you're some therapist, and you want more?"

So much more my whole body craved it

"I know you think I'm just some rich playboy—"

"You are."

"—but there's depth to me that might surprise you, Wren. I can be a good friend. Someone you can call anytime you want."

She studied me, her gaze wary. Unsure.

I fluttered the card. "Please. Accepting a small piece of paper like this can't hurt. And if you ever need someone..." I shrugged, having already made the promise in my heart and meaning every fucking word. "Whatever and wherever, okay?"

Wren tucked my card into her purse but didn't speak.

I stood and stepped to the side, allowing her access to her stairs.

She started past me but hesitated, her head lifting to

meet my gaze. Eyes red-rimmed and watery, they revealed a soul dragged through the shit, fire no person ought to face alone.

I wanted to hug her. Longed for it to the point my throat tightened. "Wren?" I whispered, not sure what I asked for or if I even did.

Her throat bobbed as she swallowed, another tear sliding down her cheek.

My arms extended—and she dropped her bag and fell against me, her tiny body wrapped up in mine. Small and warm. Sweet and crying again with heart-wrenching sobs.

Her fingers clung to the back of my shirt as though desperate to get closer. To cling and never let go.

Fuck, did I desire that.

I blinked back tears, my chin resting atop her head as she pressed her cheek against my chest. Wren fit too damn well in my arms…like she belonged there. Closing my eyes, I focused on sending comfort and good feels through my hug, enough to sustain and maybe make her not feel so damn alone.

Thank fuck my body behaved, but my heart didn't.

She had to hear my heavy beat against her cheek, the heightened pulse of an adrenaline rush from finally having her in my arms.

No skin contact.

No kissing.

No sexual touch.

But that moment meant *everything* to me.

Something clicked into place inside my chest, and I breathed easier. My feet seemed lighter. It felt like the energy of that Energizer bunny coursed through my blood, making me want to sprint up a damn mountainside.

I'd meant to comfort Wren, but it seemed she'd given me all the feels I hadn't known existed.

A heavy sigh ripped through us both at the same time. She peeled herself away from me, slowly like a kid did a Band-Aid, making me wince and wish I could yank her back and keep her there.

Wren wouldn't meet my gaze while grabbing her bag and climbing halfway up her stairs. She paused and turned, her eyes swollen behind her glasses. "Thank you. For listening—for all those notes of encouragement."

I nodded, my throat too tight at the sight of even more tears filling her eyes.

She turned and left me there, completely fucking gobsmacked and breathless with realization of how my life had taken a sudden turn.

Wren had more than burrowed under my skin. She'd weaseled her way straight into my heart.

And fuck me, I wanted in hers enough I would face heartache all over again.

Chapter 9

Wren

I sat at my kitchen table, head resting on my crossed arms atop the wooden surface, the memory of Blake's around me etched deeply into my memory. I'd been powerless to deny myself what he'd offered.

Physical comfort at one of the lowest points of my life.

He'd smelled delicious, of course, with a hint of sawdust and sweat beneath whatever soap he used, but he'd held still. Didn't grind against me. He hadn't even gotten hard—and he'd been all up against my belly enough for me to have felt that large bulge's thickened state if he'd been thinking about anything sexual.

Sighing, I pushed aside thoughts of Blake and the few moments of rest I'd allowed myself while smooshed up against his hard chest in what had seemed a sincere hug.

There were much more important shit to think on, more pressing and important distractions that would affect my plans for the rest of the summer.

Sweet darkness filled my vision, but I could still see Mom in my mind's eye, pale and wasting away on that hospital bed.

I only had two days left to myself, because once she got discharged, I would have to move into her old apartment until the end. I still wasn't sure what I would do about my job. Other than my two weeks' worth of vacation time I hadn't dipped into for the year, I had no clue how I would make things work. Not even sure of family sick time or extenuating circumstances, I floundered.

And my summer class...

"Shit." Lifting up to sit, I slowly blinked, attempting to rid my eyes and my body of absolute weariness.

First things first. Sleep. Coffee. Then call the hospital's financial department to get the money situation hopefully somewhat taken care of.

Too emotionally drained to do anything but flop onto my bed fully clothed, that was exactly what I did, and thank goodness my mind shut down so I could get some much-needed rest.

Five hours later, I woke up feeling slightly better and ready to tackle details like the stubborn woman I'd become since moving out to live on my own. Showered, two cups of coffee in me, I sat at the kitchen table and made a few phone calls, pushing for answers and settling shit in my mind.

The finances and insurance details wouldn't be settled for a few days, but at least I managed to get the ball rolling with assurance that Mom qualified for what she would need to see her through until she passed.

Throat tight at the inevitable, I next made a call to my boss at the pharmacy downtown.

Turned out, I had my vacation time but no extended family leave of any sort. If hospice allowed for any babysitting type care, I could cut back my hours with the promise of full-time for...after.

Having skipped class, my next point of business was contacting my professor with a brief explanation of my current situation. He sent along that day's notes that I had missed, but my hands were tied as far as getting to class.

Either that or drop the course and pile it atop my head for the looming school year.

What if Mom still clung to life at the end of August when my fully loaded final year fell into my daily life? As it was, I'd be lucky to get four or five hours of sleep between work and classes as it was.

Nine months until graduation. I could make it through that period of time.

I had to.

With details hammered out as well as they could be for the time being, I allowed my mind to filter back to earlier that morning.

I had unloaded on Blake regardless of my having zero plans to do so. He'd just happened to be at the wrong place at the wrong time and got an ear load of the most pitiful upbringing.

Why he'd offered his listening services if needed in the future, I had no clue, because our differences were embarrassing as hell. The man seriously wanted to get me naked.

Or maybe he's not really all that bad of a guy.

I pondered the thought, rethinking his claims of having depth, not just being some playboy wanting a good time. I'd seen the empathy on his face, could sense his displeasure—but no judgment—over Mom's many mistakes and bad choices. More than once, his hands had fisted, seemingly restless as though wanting to physically offer me comfort.

Then he had stood and pulled me into his arms. Or maybe I'd fallen into him. It had seemed we moved at the same time, but there was no doubting his whisper of my name had been empathy, not a third attempt.

But we'd been on the same wavelength and had come together.

Warmth spread through me as I remembered how he'd held me, those wide hands of his rubbing up and down my back. Nothing of a sexual nature had passed between us, just good old fashioned comfort and a sharing of emotions I'd longed for my entire life.

I eyed the card on the middle of my table, the navy font of his name and the phone number beneath luring me in like hot fudge to a premenopausal woman in need of all the good stuff.

Without giving it too much thought, I typed up a quick text message.

Me: **Thanks again for listening.**

He texted back immediately as though he'd been sitting and staring at his cell. **Anytime**.

A million nicknames flitted through my head, but I settled on his real name when adding him as a contact in my cell.

Blake: **Let me know if there's anything I can do to help.**

I huffed a teary laugh, wishing I had the balls to tell him I needed an envelope of cash instead of coffee, the next note, or whatever little gift he planned to leave on my bottom step.

Instead, I decided to let the matter rest and not text back. It would be too easy to get drawn into a distracting online conversation, and I had shit to do.

Setting my phone aside, I dove into my schoolwork, keeping my focus pointed on where it needed to be.

Myself and my future.

ℌ

Mom got sent home three days later, and shit had gotten straightened out with finances so I wouldn't be burdened by hospital bills. Hospice nurses stopped by, and were it not for Nancy, the little old lady who'd moved into the apartment next door, I would have ended up needing to drop my class and being unable to work.

A recovering addict and ten years older than my mom, Nancy appreciated the fact she'd managed to live through her younger years with the help of her old neighbors and was determined to pay it back.

Being on disability, she had government assistance. She also had the time to sit with my mom whenever I had to go out.

I hadn't been to my own apartment in three weeks other than to stop in and water my plants in the window. There were no gifts from Blake but notes aplenty—as well as texts letting me know he was thinking about me. I caved after the third, texting him a thank you, but never got caught up in messaging beyond those short exchanges. We weren't friends. Weren't anything but mere acquaintances, and I didn't have time to even consider more.

But I dreamed about him and his strong arms holding me again. Hot breath against my hair as he whispered all sorts of nonsense to me. Encouraging things, sometimes sexy.

I clung to those images in my head every morning after waking, wishing I could just disappear in dreamland for a little longer. Having thought I'd known what the word tired meant prior to Mom getting sick, I got slapped in the face with how my body dragged from place to place on stubborn will.

I longed for a hand to hold.

Physical contact that soothed like Blake's had done.

Encouragement from just not being so alone.

Mom steadily grew worse, and with my hands tied against doing more than help make her comfortable, I sometimes sat and watched her sleep.

As the end drew near, I hated how I anticipated her last breath.

I didn't really want my mom to die, but I felt sure she suffered regardless of the morphine the hospice nurse had her on. No pain, but mentally...emotionally...I wondered.

Late Saturday afternoon, she slept. Silence clung to the apartment, and I restlessly set to cleaning up another section of the mess she had lived in for years.

A hoarder to some extent, she piled up shit everywhere. At least it wasn't trash and old food, causing mildew and the stench of filth. But, still.

Books. Magazines. Clothes. Trinkets from who the hell knew where—full-on collections of shit she hadn't owned when I had lived at home. It was like she had grabbed up the boxes labeled *FREE* on sidewalks after yard or garage sales.

It would take a full-sized dumpster to rid the place of her junk when the time came.

I wanted to guzzle a bottle of wine until drunk and just forget my reality.

Getting laid would be a great release too.

Escaping from reality for a while even better.

Shit, all three sounded absolutely delicious. I definitely couldn't do the first since I had to keep my wits about me just in case, but the other two?

While showering in the bathroom I'd had to Clorox the hell out of after moving in to care for Mom, I actually considered an hour or two of selfishness losing myself in distracting release.

And I knew exactly how to go about getting it.

While I kept faith in the red flags I'd seen about Blake, I also...trusted him in some ways after that day at the foot of my apartment stairs. He'd proven he wasn't just after me for sex. He'd been empathetic. Understanding.

My suspicion radar should have been on high alert telling me he'd only done so to weasel his way into my pants, but I found my defenses lowered.

No doubt he could give me what I needed, and I could definitely shut shit down on the emotions front and just enjoy the release he would give me.

Especially if a third wheel was involved.

The stirrings of excitement rose inside my chest for the first time in longer than I could remember as I considered allowing myself something frivolous for a change.

It felt damn near necessary as I teetered on the edge of exhaustion or a breakdown.

My heartbeat sped up as I called the neighbor, Nancy. She wasn't doing more than watching TV and was happy to give me the night off. Her telling me I deserved a break lessened my guilt over what I planned to do.

I sat on the edge of the single mattress pushed against my old bedroom wall surrounded by stuff and studied Blake's contact information.

A Saturday night...what were the chances he wasn't already balls deep in some random blonde bimbo? Or out drinking with his friends? No man that hot, that luscious-looking would be sitting around on the weekend twiddling his thumbs.

But it couldn't hurt to find out.

Biting down on the inside of my lip, I did what I told myself I would never do no matter how desperate I grew for physical touch.

I gave into my body's needs rather than using my brain and set about to fulfilling one of my fantasies.

Merely for escape.

Chapter 10

Blake

Micah talked me into being eye candy along with Jarod, one of his employees, and once more desperate, he'd begged Reid to join us. Since all he had to do was look good and eat gourmet food, Reid had agreed to tag along for the ride but only because he had nothing and no one better to do.

I'd become the Renshaw's regular voyeur, but that was all I'd given Micah until that night. Heart set on Wren, I refused to touch anyone else but didn't mind watching that couple love on each other.

She hadn't initiated any conversations over the previous couple of weeks and rarely answered with more than a word or two whenever I checked in with her. I continued to leave her little notes on her stairs too, the longing to just be there for her more important than my dick's lack of action beyond my hand.

I'd never felt that way before, but that tiny woman... yeah. I wanted to give her all the flowers and whisk her away on a tropical vacation where she would have no choice but to relax. Buy her diamonds and designer clothes. Share expensive wine and stare all heart-eyed at her over some table at a five-star restaurant.

Because of my little birdie, I refused to consider myself an Elite Escort like Jarod.

He, Reid, and I stood at the open bar in one of Boston's swanky hotel's ball rooms. We'd been hired by some rich dude with three daughters to act as their dates for some overseas dignitary's son's wedding reception. Most of the guests were foreign, and even the dates we'd been assigned hardly spoke English.

Pretending to party it up with the ridiculously wealthy, the three of us stuck to soda and seltzers, alcohol being off-limits to Micah's men while on the job.

"Are all eye candy jobs this damn boring?" Reid muttered while leaning against the bar and checking out the mingling guests.

We'd caught a rare moment alone, huddled up like true introverts of which none a one of us could claim to be. It'd been a long-as-fuck four hours since the event had started, and I was ready to get the fuck out of there and go grab a couple beers.

"Sometimes," Jarod replied. "These types of contracts aren't nearly as satisfying as fucking."

"Don't you get tired of it?" Reid asked, turning to face Jarod. "Constant pussy for free? Fuck. Getting *paid* for the use of your dick?"

"Nope." He grinned, his dark eyes assessing my best friend. "Micah's been after you to work for him, hasn't he?"

"Every damn chance he gets, he's all up in my space," Reid replied. "I'm starting to think he has the hots for me."

"His brother might but not Micah. He has no interest in dick."

"Are there any bi or gay escorts on his payroll?" I asked, just looking to make conversation to pass the time.

"Not yet, but his brother has been on his ass to expand that way," Jarod said.

"Who would pay for gay sex when there's apps for free hookups?" Reid asked.

Jarod shrugged. "I don't know shit about the business. I just get texted a file and contract, either take the job or decline, and call it a day. Like I said—easy."

We stood silent for a few minutes, just shy of twiddling our thumbs.

"He gets requests for twins sometimes," Jarod told Reid. "Seeing as how you and I could pass for brothers, I'm not surprised he wants you on his payroll. I'm his most requested, so having basically two of us? Bank, baby."

Reid glanced over at me, a clear question in his eyes.

"Don't look to me for advice," I said, lifting a hand in a stop gesture. "You're one hell of a wingman and pussy whisperer. Damn near worth your weight in gold in all ways as far as I'm concerned. And we've shared enough women for me to promise you'd make one hell of an escort too."

Reid studied his drink for a bit, and I eyed my Rolex.

One long as fuck hour to go.

"Personally," I continued, "I don't know what's holding you back. All you do is chase after your next hookup anyway."

Not that he had to try all that hard. His brawn and good looks got him women's attention without too much effort.

"Why not relax, let someone else do the work for you, *and* get paid for it," I continued. "Just don't go leaving your day job. Then I'd have to kick your ass for real."

"You don't think it's...well." Reid waved his hand as

though we'd read his mind—which I definitely did having known him most of my life.

Jarod snorted before I could reply. "People do what people gotta do, man. Besides, it's easy money. Add this income atop my day job as a nurse, and I'm on track to retire before I hit forty."

"Get the fuck out," Reid said, both of his eyebrows raised.

"Nope." Jarod took a sip of his soda and set his glass on the bar behind him. "That's what happens when you do this as long as I have and watch what you spend."

Jarod had been with Micah since the beginning of EE—so over a decade of fucking for money.

And Wren thought I had a few too many notches on my bed post.

But to each their own. I didn't give a fuck what people did to earn a living, nor would I ever judge someone for enjoying sex to the fullest.

The conversation dropped, and the circumstances made for one boring night, but at least the food had been good. We'd agreed to hit a bar afterward, but all I could think about was Wren sitting by her mom—if the woman even still lived.

I hated that Wren didn't keep me posted on how her mom fared but had to admit to myself that although she'd shared the burden of her childhood emotions with me, she didn't see me as a friend. And definitely not something more regardless of how badly I desired it.

After one final dance where I held my date lightly and attempted conversation, the reception dwindled down.

Five minutes.

I'd had my fill of soda water. Fancy food like Mom and Dad always had at their parties. I'd also reached my limits for fake smiles and pretending to listen to conversations I couldn't even understand.

Jarod and Reid seemed just as antsy to leave, unbuttoning suit coats and loosening ties.

We said our goodbyes and headed to the exit the second nine o'clock rolled around.

"O'Malley's?" Jarod suggested as Reid and I both pulled our cells from our pockets since being on Micah's clock meant no phones in hand for the duration of work hours too.

I stumbled to a stop outside the hotel, Wren's name glowing on my screen. A grin split my face initially but perhaps her mom...

I clicked on the message.

Stared.

Reread her words, sure I hadn't understood the first time.

"What's up?" Jarod asked me when I didn't move from where I'd halted in the middle of the sidewalk.

"Change of plans," I said, my heart speeding up so damn fast my mouth dried out. My fingers flew over the screen.

Be there in thirty, I promised.

I met Reid's gaze. "Would you believe me if I said Wren just invited the two of us over to her apartment to fulfill her threesome fantasy?"

He laughed. "No fucking way."

"I'm serious." Every cell in my body buzzed. "Sorry, Jarod, but we gotta jet."

"Who says I'm in the mood to see your dick tonight?" Reid asked, his dark eyes full of shit. "Maybe I'd rather sit with Jarod and talk about loaning my body out to horny women."

"Don't you dare let me down at this opportunity of a fucking lifetime!"

"Wren is the girl you've been hung up on, huh?" Jarod asked.

"Yeah."

"According to Micah, you'll never give up the playboy lifestyle. What about this girl makes her different?" he asked.

I couldn't explain it. Didn't have words for how she made me crave things beyond the physical. A connection was what I wanted, like my parents shared. But I never imagined such a relationship might be for me.

Wren had invited me and Reid over for purely physical interaction, a distraction, an escape from the shit I could imagine piled up on her shoulders.

She hadn't said yes to a date. Hadn't agreed to get to know me better or offered me a chance to lay the real me bare for her to judge and laugh at.

But she *had* given me an in, and I wasn't about to fuck it up.

"Reid," I pleaded, ready to give whatever it would take to get him to be my wingman for the night.

He studied me in the street lights, his gaze wary. "You're actually gonna let me touch her? Kiss her? Fuck her?"

I'd shared so many women with Reid and never had jealousy issues before, but I'd never been emotionally caught up in any of them either.

"You can have whatever piece of her she wants to share with you," I told him, my mind made up on pleasing Wren —no matter how possessive I felt myself growing deep inside my guts.

"You sure about that?" Reid asked quietly, his dark eyes assessing my face.

"Yeah." I nodded while settling that shit in my head even though my heart screamed no. "Whatever Wren wants, she gets."

He nodded but didn't grin like he usually would have. "Then let's go please your little birdie."

Chapter 11

Wren

I hadn't just asked Blake for his dick—I'd requested that buffer he'd suggested weeks ago too. Having a second body to focus on would keep my emotions behind lock and key where they needed to stay.

The last thing I needed was to fall for someone like him, lose my heart, and add even more bullshit atop what I faced in the year ahead.

I'd sent the invite and, without waiting for answer, had driven north to my own apartment. Even if Blake and his buddy weren't available, I planned on spending the night away from the smell of death and stifling silence.

While my meager belongings and the house I lived in showcased my financial state to someone who probably used twenty dollar bills to blow his nose, I couldn't afford a hotel room for our hookup.

I told myself I didn't care what he thought about me. My lack, my less-than compared to him and his family.

I only wanted his dick.

Okay, so his arms and hands too.

But not his mouth. Definitely not. That would be too

intimate for how drawn I already was to him. Tasting his tongue would be dangerous for my heart.

I enjoyed a single glass of wine while lounging on the couch and treating myself to a good menage book by my favorite author, Annie Kelly. The woman knew how to write spice and get a woman's insides heated up with her vivid descriptions of two men loving on a woman.

Being the sole focus of two mouths and four hands—

My cell dinged, and my heart sped up.

Could be selfishly great news or some of the worst sort from Nancy...

Blake: **Be there in thirty.**

"Oh my God, I'm doing this." I swallowed hard, my stomach a mess of jitters. Eyeing my empty wine glass, I put through a call to Mom's neighbor to check on them.

Mom hadn't eaten much of the soup I'd set out for her and had already fallen back to sleep.

Hand shaking, I poured myself another glass of wine, too damn worked up over the decision I'd made to face it stone-cold sober. Having barely eaten anything for dinner, that second glass I sucked down in twenty minutes left me decently buzzed and left me feeling more confident than I'd hoped for.

I heard a car pull up in front of the house. Two doors slamming. Footsteps climbing my stairs.

Blowing out a slow, steady exhale didn't lessen my nervousness, but I made my way to the door, my chin lifted.

This is just a hookup. An escape from the shit of my life for a while. What he thinks about my apartment doesn't matter.

The sight of Blake on my stoop hit me like a fist to the temple must feel.

Rattled.

Dizzy.

Unable to think past the effects the sight of him brought on.

Head lowered, he lifted his focus to my face—as though attempting to make himself appear smaller, less intimidating, would actually work. He dwarfed me.

And I loved it.

A suit coat stretched over his wide shoulders, navy blue —the same color as his expressive eyes. Loosened tie, the top two buttons undone.....

My core purred over the thought of exploring all the smooth skin beneath, mussing his perfect hair, biting his plump lower lip.

No. Not that.

But yes to having those big, capable hands running over my body.

His slow smirk revealed his dimple, damn him, and I swallowed a rush of drool while fighting off tremors.

"Hey there, little birdie," he murmured, drawing me out of lust-hazed fog.

"Sorry," I whispered, stepping back and opening the door to let him inside.

He moved past me, and I breathed in the scent of his spicy cologne, every inch of my skin tingling.

Another person shifted in my periphery, and I jerked my head toward the stoop, having completely forgotten about the second man I'd insisted he bring along.

"Wren, Reid," Blake introduced us. "Reid, my little birdie."

I shot Blake a glare for the possessive word he'd tossed in there but immediately turned back to his friend.

As expected, Reid was the man I'd watched when Blake had been absent on the jobsite. Tall, dark, and handsome, he looked like he spent just as much time in the gym as Blake, his slow smile was just as lethal.

That man would prove dangerous to any woman's libido.

I held out a shaking hand, and Reid's warm clasp slid warmth down my spine to settle between my thighs.

Yeah, I was in for one hell of a night of glorious, debauched, thought-erasing release.

Shivering regardless of the night's warmth, I shut the door behind Reid, gladly sealing my fate for the next couple of hours.

"Can I get either of you a beer?" I croaked. "Glass of wine?"

Blake's eyebrows shot up, but a wide grin quickly replaced his surprise. "I'd love a beer."

He'd thought I would tell them to strip the second they walked into my place—but why wouldn't he? I'd never shown interest in getting to know him, and while that wasn't my intent in inviting him over, I wasn't sure exactly how to proceed with getting a threesome underway.

"Reid?" I asked.

"Sure."

"Make yourselves at home," I said, heading on weak legs into the small kitchen where I took a few more deep breaths to calm the jitters attempting to wreck my insides.

For once, I would have the sexcapade stories to share at work. Jenny would be damn proud of me.

Holding back a snicker, I went back to the living room, their beers in hand.

Blake had made himself at home on my old, sagging couch, all sprawled out and appearing a lot more comfortable in my apartment than I was with him being there.

Handing over his drink, I couldn't decide how I felt about that observance.

The man obviously decided he belonged in my personal space, and I admitted to myself that he looked damn good being there regardless of the old red flags waving off in the distance.

"Thanks," he murmured, his voice like silky sex, all molten chocolate and sweet in my ears.

I held back my snort. "You're welcome."

Reid moved through the room as though restless, checking out every trinket I'd received from his boss and best friend.

He turned when I approached, his dark eyes caressing down my neck to the gentle swell of my small breasts beneath my tank top. My nipples hardened, and he smiled, seeming just as ease as Blake with how I'd propositioned them.

"Here." I thrust the beer toward him, wishing I had another glass of wine to guzzle. I blurted the first thought that came to mind that didn't involve tongues, fingers, or holes. "Sorry if Blake dragged your ass here and ruined your plans for the night."

He turned toward me, stepping in close and watching my eyes. "I didn't have any. And I'll gladly do whatever you want, Wren. Whatever you need."

Strangely, I trusted his words. Perhaps it was because I hadn't stalked him online and hadn't made assumptions before speaking to him.

Shifting my stance, that damn thought wanted to expand into guilt, but I pushed it aside at the feel of Blake's stare on my backside.

I gave Reid my full attention rather than turning.

He stood just as gorgeous, but there was less of the draw

I always felt around Blake. I took in the tall drink of water from dark hair to shiny dress shoes, soaking in the beauty of his flawless skin, perfectly formed lips, and chiseled jawline.

A dark god, and I knew from seeing him in tight T-shirts all sweaty at work, he was hot as hell beneath his black suit that stretched over muscles too.

"What comes to mind when you look at me like that?" he murmured, reaching out to brush some of my hair over my shoulder.

I loved how Reid took the lead while Blake sat quiet behind us. Shivers slid over me as his fingertips caressed my skin. No sizzle raced over my skin at his touch, but it was... alluring all the same.

He seemed like a good man. Sturdy. Hardworking and responsible. But he'd cameoed in Blake's social media.

"If I hadn't seen a few online pics of you hugging up on the other side of Blake's blonde bimbos, I would say you swing a hammer by day and make one lucky woman feel cherished every night," I stated with absolute assurance in my tone.

Blake barked with laughter.

"What?" I asked, pivoting to face him, my hands on my hips. "Reid seems like the loyal, one-woman-man type. Unlike you," I threw in for good measure as he laughed again.

"If anyone deserves the name playboy, it's Sully," Blake said, still smirking.

I tossed a glance over my shoulder at Reid whose last name I guessed to be Sullivan. My eyesight took a bit to catch up with my head, telling me that second glass of wine I'd drained had hit my empty stomach harder than expected.

"Well?" I asked Reid, giving him a chance to defend himself.

"I thoroughly enjoy sampling in my quest to find *the one*," he said with a shrug.

Rolling my eyes, I shook my head. Yeah, I'd definitely chosen the right men to give me the kind of night I needed.

There would be no pining. No longing outside getting off.

"What do you want tonight, Wren?" Blake asked, but I didn't know how to respond other than with brutal honesty.

"To forget about life for a couple hours. I just need to feel, not think. Nothing more. Can you give me that?"

His gaze softened, the sensitivity in his eyes same as that morning he'd hugged me, hitting all my feels.

My eyes stung, but I held his stare, shutting down the steel doors to my heart in determination to stay purely physical with him.

"Come here, little bird." Setting aside his drink, he held out his hand.

I went willingly, thinking I might have signed my soul over to the devil...

At the caress of his palm over mine, the thought turned to fact as I went pliant as putty.

Big fucking red flags waved, an alarm blaring *alert* at my stupid plan, but I was too far gone. Desire for escape led my steps, and I trusted the two playboys to take me there.

Chapter 12

Blake

Reid could sport wood at the drop of a hat. His dress pants revealed exactly what he thought of Wren in her little sleep shorts and tank top. I'd finally gotten an eyeful of what lay beneath her work clothes, and I was far from disappointed. Definitely less curvy than my norm—those tall blondes she griped about twice since having met her—but that tangible thing between us lured me in.

The sight of her eyes hazing over.

The slight tremble of her lower lip.

The way she so easily came to me, taking my hand in what seemed like complete trust.

I was fucking done for.

That was what swelled my dick. Not the promise of a wet pussy or having a woman writhe between me and my best friend. Nothing but a deep yearning to fulfill her needs excited every damn cell in my body.

A strange sensation but the opposite of unpleasant.

I'd planned to pull her onto my lap and devour her mouth, but I knew once I got a taste of her exhales, the softness of her submitting to my lips, I would be desperate for more, things I doubted she would ever give me.

Wren only wanted to fuck. She'd made that clear in her text. Letting myself get caught up in emotions would lead to a sure broken heart.

I stood and turned her, pulling her back against my body so she faced Reid who studied my face over her head as she sagged against me, already boneless.

We'd shared so many women, had been best friends for so many years that sometimes we were able to communicate in silence. Hoping he saw the conflicting thoughts I had inside, I nodded for him to take the lead.

He moved in without preamble or words, bent to sit his barely touched beer on the end table, and tugged Wren's tank top up and over her head.

Goose bumps broke over her body, and I splayed my hands around her warm skin, damn near spanning her waist. Her head tipped to the side at my first exhale over her clavicle, the barest hint of a whimper bucking my dick inside my slacks. Needing more noises, I set on nips with my teeth, tonguing over the gentle bites.

Reid shed his suit coat and tie, his focus on her face the entire time. Off went his shoes, and seconds later, he crowded Wren between us.

His hands went to her face, and I reminded myself we were there for her—whatever she desired.

Closing my eyes, I buried my face in the back of her neck and slid my hands into the sides of her shorts. So damn silky and warm.

The sounds of kissing raged a war in my heart of wanting to be possessive, but I swallowed my envy over Reid tasting her mouth, focusing on caressing her body as she stayed pliant in our arms. She'd gone without panties, and I groaned, a tremor rippling over me.

My fingers slid along the insides of her thighs beneath her shorts, the heat of her core radiating. Enticing. Beckoning me to touch.

Thoughts of how to fulfill her needs flitted through my mind, all with the two of us face to face, eye-fucking as deeply as I would her body. But there was no way I could look into her troubled orbs and not fall into her and lose my soul.

I would keep the perfect third wheel in her line of sight.

"Bedroom?" I whispered against her ear, regretfully removing my touch from beneath her shorts.

She gulped and nodded.

Reid straightened and laced his fingers through hers while I trailed along behind as she led him toward the second door along a short hallway. I rid my upper body of clothes as I went.

Shirtless, I stood inside her bedroom door and kicked off my shoes, gaze glued to her cute, little ass as Reid pulled her sleep shorts down.

Neither Reid nor Wren spoke, but when she glanced over her shoulder, she stole my breath, making words impossible. Hunger radiated in her stare as she took me in from my bare chest to the dress pants I'd stalled out in unzipping.

She licked her lower lip…waiting.

Fuck.

The curse groaned through my head, and my hands shook while shoving down my pants and briefs. My hard dick slapped against my belly at its release.

"Oh my god," she whisper-moaned, her face flushed.

Pride rushed through me as I kicked off my pants, and I

palmed my dick, smearing the droplet of pre-cum down my length.

Reid finished undressing while Wren ogled me, and I stayed out of arm's reach even though I wanted to rush in and devour her exactly in the way her eyes stated she lusted for.

She swallowed hard and lifted her focus to my face. Dark, luminous pupils ate at the hazel of her irises behind those sexy as hell glasses.

"Take them off," I said, my voice nothing but strangled need as I motioned toward her face.

Her hands shook as she removed her glasses, and I held out my hand. She placed them on my palm, the graze of her fingertips sending a shot of need to my dick.

I nodded at Reid who clasped her hips and turned her back toward him. Setting aside her glasses on the bureau, I inhaled deeply, attempting to settle my nerves. A quick fish through my pants pocket while Reid kissed Wren's mouth filled my hand with the supplies I'd brought along.

Two condoms. Lube in the event she wanted to take us both at the same time.

Reid sat on the edge of her bed, holding her face in his hands again while devouring her mouth.

Teeth clenched against the churn in my stomach, I tossed the condoms and lube packet onto the mattress beside him, crowding in close against Wren's backside.

My hard dick pressed against the small of her back, rippling a shudder through her.

She tore her mouth from Reid's and angled her head up and back to catch my gaze.

"How do you want us?" I asked, my tone raspy as fuck, letting Reid know I'd about reached the end of my restraint. And I hadn't even gotten a taste of more than her neck.

I slid my hands around her, thumbs grazing over her stiff nipples. Less than a handful of flesh fitted against my palms, but I loved how responsive she was to my touch.

She cursed softly, eyelids fluttering shut as she arched into me as though desperate for my hands to trace over every inch of her skin.

"I-I don't know. I've never been with two guys at the same time," she whispered as I continued to make her writhe with my fingertips alone. "God, that feels so damn good."

Still plucking at her tight nub, I moved my other hand down over her pert backside, my fingertips trailing through her crack. "Anyone have you here before?" I asked while rubbing over her soft puckered hole.

She swallowed hard and nodded.

"Can I?"

"Yes," she whispered, and Jesus fucking Christ, that word...

Pre-cum leaked from my dick as I nuzzled against her hair, attempting to calm my racing heart.

"Does your fantasy involve a dick here at the same time?" Reid asked while reaching between her thighs.

Wren shuddered against my chest as he fingered her, a whimpered moan rolling past her lips. "Mmm hmm."

Not a yes but consent.

Catching Reid's gaze, I tipped my chin toward the condom.

He suited up and laid back, legs dangling off the edge of Wren's bed. "Come here, sweet girl."

Reid was no small boy, but I expected she could take him without any effort. But shoving another cock inside her a membrane of skin away from him? It would be a tight as fuck squeeze, one that might make my balls explode before her heat fully engulfed me.

Shivering, Wren climbed atop Reid to straddle his waist, and he drew her down, hands sliding along her spine to grab hold of her ass. She rubbed against his core, leaving a smear of arousal over his lower abs.

Her hair cascaded around them but did nothing to hide the sounds of wet kissing. Once more attempting to ignore how my stomach tightened over my best friend tasting the mouth I wanted to own, I dropped to my knees. I guided her body backward until the tip of his dick slid over her lower pink lips. Their mouths separated due to their height difference. I couldn't kiss her, but I could make myself feel better by being the person to gift Reid her wet pussy.

He notched—and slid partway in with one slow, upward thrust.

Wren moaned and shuddered.

Envious as fuck of my best friend, I smoothed my hands over her ass cheeks, mouth watering as Reid rolled his hips, slowly fucking his length fully into her.

Lucky fucking bastard. I hated he could love on her in the ways I longed to do.

"Okay, sweetheart?" Reid asked her, rubbing his hands over the pale skin of her back.

"Mmm," she hummed, shifting her hips to take him to the root.

Not much space existed between her puckered hole and where Reid filled her, but I shoved my face in anyway, needing a taste.

Reid and I had never crossed swords or lines when sharing a woman, but my chin rubbed over his shaft as I licked up over her puckered hole.

If he minded, tough shit. I needed the flavor of her in my mouth, the scent of her in my nose.

Wren was pure musk and sweetness, so goddamned delicious, and I shoved my tongue into her ass, loving how her cheeks clenched in my hands.

"Taste so fucking good," I murmured and lapped, swirling and probing until she whimpered.

Sitting back on my heels, heart pounding, I grabbed the lube and second condom.

My gaze latched on the tight rosebud I wanted to shove inside while I sheathed up.

Soon.

I poured lube down her ass crack, enough it dripped onto Reid's balls below.

She shuddered, and he cursed at the cool slickness.

My fingers replaced my tongue on her hole, gently rubbing while Reid continued to slowly fuck up into her, his hands all fisted in her hair as she rested her forehead on his chest.

"Relax," I murmured, dipping my fingertip into her tight heat.

She bore down instead, sucking my entire finger deep into her ass like she was starved for me.

"Fuck," I groaned, her silken walls so damn tight heat flushed through me. Swallowing hard, I worked my finger in opposition to Reid's dick, filling her in a perfect rhythm that quickly had her panting.

"More." Her quiet demand flooded me with the desire to give her whatever the fuck she wanted.

She got a second finger, and I took my time stretching her.

One hand grasping her cheek wider, I watched Reid's

cream-covered dick shunt in and out of her, the soft pink skin of her pucker accepting my fingers with ease.

I worked in a third, and a noise of discomfort leaked past her lips.

Reid's hips went still as he soothed his hands up and down her back. "Shh. Relax, Wren. We'll make it good for you. Promise."

I pressed in deeper, twisting my wrist.

"Oh God." She gulped and shuddered as I placed a kiss on her ass cheek.

"Okay?" I asked, running my free hand down the outside of her smooth thigh.

"Y-yeah. I-I think." She blew out a breath and rested her cheek on Reid's pec. "Don't stop."

No fucking way I could have.

I slid my fingers from her hole, leaving it slightly gaped. "Christ, Wren. Fuck." I pushed them back in, the wet squelch of lube and the heat of her welcoming my touch making my eyes roll back in my head. "I need inside you so damn bad. Been dreaming about it for fucking ever."

"Yes."

That word again…

I pulled my fingers from her hold and crowded in close. "Let me in, little birdie."

Chapter 13

Wren

Reid already stuffed me near to bursting, and Blake's thick fingers?

Holy hell, I was going to pop from the intense pressure of being too full. I sagged in relief when his touch left my ass but couldn't calm my racing pulse or panted breaths.

Reid's heart beat near in time with mine beneath my ear, and I clenched my eyelids tight, thoroughly focused on Blake shifting behind us. What he did. What he thought. What pleasure he would take in finally having me.

I'd never been so turned on in my life. An embarrassing amount of arousal slickened between my thighs, but Reid didn't seem to care I'd probably made a mess all over his balls.

The blunt head of Blake's dick pressed lightly against my backdoor, and his warm hands enclosed over my hips, grounding me slightly.

This is it. I exhaled slowly, forcing myself to relax. *Let that sexy man have access to what he's been after since day one. Let him give you what your body and soul crave—*

"Let me in, Wren," he murmured a plea and pushed.

"Oh shit!" I tensed up on instinct from the pain, but also the double meaning I swore I heard in his voice.

He backed off, his soft lips trailing down my spine as Reid's hands continued to rub my sides.

"Fuck. Sorry," I muttered.

They both murmured quiet words of encouragement while I breathed deeply, trying like hell to keep my mind on the physical rather than the pull I felt toward the man kneeling behind me.

My intense need from seconds earlier had definitely ebbed, but I was nothing if not stubborn. "Try again. Please."

Blake held my hips steady. "Bear down," he murmured, his dick once more pressing lightly against my hole.

I exhaled and did as told, a deep, guttural groan rising from my chest as he slipped past my tight ring.

Holy fucking Christ on a goddamned cracker, he was thick.

I gulped. Panted, restless against Reid's hard chest as the truth of having Blake Harper invading my body swept luscious chills through me.

Purely physical, I reminded myself, keeping my focus on the pain rather than the longing for a deeper connection.

Both men continued to keep their hips still, petting over me with soothing touches, their soft murmurs of encouragement lost to my ears. All my concentration on the stinging stretch, the feeling of being too damn full of cock, I couldn't thoroughly enjoy the calloused palms and fingertips liberally giving me what I'd craved since my last boyfriend.

Sweat broke out on my forehead, the heat of Reid's body becoming too much.

I pushed up onto shaking arms to create some distance in my mind, head hanging. "G-give me more," I whispered, my mouth dry as dust.

"I have you." Blake pushed, and I bore down again, immediately realizing the worst was over. Thickness slid deeper in my ass, and I groaned again as my body gave way without a lick of pain.

A hiss sounded from behind me as Blake's hold on my hips tightened. "So damn tight," he groaned. "Fuck, Wren."

Reid's hands found my breasts, the sharpness of his fingernails dragging over my furled nipples and sending zinging bolts of electricity straight to my clit.

"Oh God," I moaned, my head lifting.

Pupils blown, he peered at me with those chocolate brown eyes, a furrow between his brows. "Okay?"

Blake backed out, and I shuddered as he slid in again, gaining ground deep inside my ass.

"Uh huh," I managed as goose bumps rose all over me at my body giving him access.

"Come here," Reid murmured, lifting onto his elbows and curling upward to touch his lips to mine. His hand cradled the back of my neck, and I rested some of my weight on his chest as he slid his tongue into my mouth.

He tasted of hops, and his ability to kiss stole some of my focus off the double intrusion.

Blake continued to work inside with gentle, slow strokes. "Such a good girl," he said, the sexy rasp of his voice sliding over my skin like delicious AC on the hottest day. "You took every inch of me, Wren—you're so fucking perfect."

I sighed heavily, sinking onto Reid's chest as he laid back once more.

Blake leaned forward over us, his lips on my nape where Reid held my hair out of his way. "So sweet." He licked over my ear, sending shivers up my spine, one hand sliding from my shoulder to my hip. "Beautiful."

He shifted away from me, dragging his dick from me until only his glans kept him nestled inside my tight ring of muscles. "Reid."

One wordless command, but the boys didn't need to communicate any more than that.

Reid pulled out as Blake pushed back in.

Fire erupted over my skin, and I whimpered at the exquisite, erotic opposing glides in my body.

"Good?" Blake checked in with me as he bottomed out, his breath warm on my ear.

"So, so good," I said. My life would never be the same. The fantasy of having two dicks inside me didn't compare to the reality of buzzing tension stringing me tight. My entire core throbbed. My clit ached as their movements caused the swollen flesh to rub over Reid's pelvis.

I would come untouched.

No doubt.

"More," I heard myself beg, uncaring of my needy tone, completely lost to everything but the push and pull, the drag of slick hardness shoving in and out of me.

Something coiled deep inside me, a clenching sensation that promised glorious release.

My harsh pants ghosted over Reid's chest as the two of them went faster. Deeper.

Reid groaned, his entire body rocking hard beneath me with every flex of his hips. "She's so hot and tight around my dick, Blake. Fucking hell I'm close."

Rubbing my forehead against Reid, I attempted to shift between their heat, chasing what I needed.

Blake didn't give me his weight, but I felt like him like a furnace, mere inches from my skin. I wanted him to crash into me. Pin me down against Reid. Fuck me raw until I couldn't walk for days...

He sat back and grabbed hold of my hips, his own quickly losing rhythm. "Make her come," he groaned out.

"Fuck yeah." Reid slid a hand between our bodies, and the second his fingertips grazed over my clit, I shuddered.

"Oh *god*," I rasped with a gasped moan as my core spasmed around them both.

"Yes," Blake hissed, his pelvis slamming against my ass cheeks as he pounded into me over and over again. "Take your pleasure from us, baby. Take us with you."

Eyes clenched tight, I wailed as my climax swept through my core like a tsunami, wave after undulating wave slamming into me. I pulsed around their thrusting cocks, choking on gasps for air. A continuous slew of curses fell from my lips as I attempted to arch and curl inward at the same time.

Sensory overload.

Too much.

"Fuck." Reid's dick throbbed inside me as he came, his arms banded around my back, squeezing the life from me.

My heart pounded, ears ringing, soaking in how he came undone beneath me—but I needed more. I lusted for Blake to lose himself. Craved hearing the sounds he made as he climaxed.

"Blake," I whispered on a moan, begging for him to take what he'd been after since the day we'd met.

"Jesus, Wren." Blake shoved in deep, his hands in a bruising grip on my hips. His dick bucked inside me, his guttural groan rumbling in my ears and causing another shudder to ripple through my core.

Gulping over the perfection of his body, the noises leaving his lips at having found release with me, I sagged against his best friend.

My body lay sated, and my mind quiet for the first time in weeks.

𝕴𝕴

I slowly woke from a deep, dreamless sleep, groaning as I shoved my face deeper into my pillow.

The night before rushed back into my mind.

I barely remembered a warm wet rag wiping between my thighs, the bed dipping on either side of me...

Heat and hard bodies still pressed against my front and back.

They had stayed.

A hint of early morning sunlight filtered around the edges of my bedroom's blinds, creating just enough light I could make out the deep blue of Blake's eyes inches from mine.

"Good morning." His rumbled words sped arousal straight through my body, waking tingles through my aching core.

"Mmm," I hummed an agreement, wanting to curse over the fact he looked so damn at home in my bed.

And I definitely liked seeing him there.

He rubbed a thumb over the groove in my forehead. "Did we hurt you?"

"No, but don't get any ideas about a second helping anytime soon," I muttered more for my own sake than his.

A slow smirk popped his damned dimple.

I huffed and turned onto my back rather than giving into my desire to kiss those perfect lips of his.

He hadn't kissed me the night before, had almost seem to...orchestrate our entire affair, making sure Reid stayed in front of me which I had appreciated.

I refused to consider the whys outside my own. His reason for doing so didn't matter since this was a one-and-done like we both had expected from my finally giving in, the perfect distraction.

Lips touched both my shoulders at the same time, morning wood quickly snuggling in tight against my lower legs.

"Don't get any ideas," I whispered, closing my eyes in an attempt to hide from the reality creeping into my brain.

Hands ran over my body beneath the sheets, making my nipples ache and core drip.

Damn magic—both of them. I soaked that shit up, tucking away the memories of callouses and fingertips gliding over me for when I once more grew starved for physical touch.

Within minutes I panted, restless as their pre-cum smeared against my skin.

Reid lifted, his mouth closing over my breast.

I moaned, grabbing hold of his hair as his teeth nibbled on my nipple. "Have mercy," I whispered.

"No way, sweet girl." He bit again, and Blake shifted, pushing my thighs wide to make way for his shoulders.

"Ung," a grunt ripped from me as he licked up through my swollen lower lips.

"So damn sweet," he murmured before taking another slow taste, his tongue dipping into my core. "Fuck, Wren. I could eat your pussy for hours."

A shudder rippled over me at his filthy words and my intense desire for him to do that very thing.

I'd only planned on giving them one climax, but another stole up on me as Blake's lips closed over my clit.

A few flicks of his tongue in time with Reid's on my nipple, and I came with a cry, bucking beneath them. Shuddering uncontrollably. Shivering with that same sense of overload that had blown my mind the night before.

"Oh god. Holy shit." I gulped, slowing settling as they lathed their tongues over my flesh, gently helping me come back from the intense orgasm.

They landed gentle kisses on me and then both backed away.

I lay spent. Arms and legs askew, hair probably a rat's nest, every inch of me flushed. Eyes closed, I basked in the afterglow, the distraction from reality as long as I could.

Reid rolled away first, his weight leaving the bed.

I listened as he used the bathroom, too aware of the one still beside me. His heat was a magnet. The desire for more of his touch was the same damn tractor beam as when our gazes had first met but ten times as strong.

Unlike the night before when I'd been trapped between two bodies, I needed to shy away from Blake. To escape the pull—

He moved into a plank over my body, the weight of him on my lower half pinning me in place. But he felt like a soothing blanket I wanted to curl up beneath. Lose myself in.

It would be so damn easy to just let go.

But the end result of a broken heart wouldn't do a damn thing in helping to sustain me for the months ahead.

Mentally releasing a heavy exhale to center myself, I forced my eyelids up to take in his lustful gaze.

Inches away, Blake stared down at me with tenderness, the warmth in his navy blues slamming that sense of connection into place, the same I'd felt when he'd held me in his arms and I'd wet his shirt with my tears.

Longing rose inside me, so damn intense I couldn't breathe. Wetness hazed the vision of him. I swallowed hard, determined to keep him at arm's length even though our skin touched from waist to toes, and something inside me gently whispered it would be alright.

Give in. Kiss him.

His stare flitted to my mouth but back up just as quickly.

I knew he wouldn't want more, but I didn't trust myself to not get lost and lose sight of all I had planned for my life. Blake Harper might be a god worth worshiping, but I couldn't afford to bend a knee.

He had been a beautiful distraction, but our time together had ended.

Clearing my throat, I tore my focus off his to glance at the windows, ignoring the lone tear sliding down my cheek to drip onto my bed.

Early morning sunlight filtered around the blinds, a stark reminder of the new day ahead. "You should go." My tone held more force than I'd hoped for.

"Wren."

Nope. Nuh uh.

I closed my eyes and set my lips in a thin line.

"Wren," he pushed with a hint of pleading in his voice, but I refused to give him my eyes, let alone a piece of my heart.

"No," I whispered as another tear leaked from beneath my lashes.

Heavy silence stifled the air between us.

The toilet flushed. The sink ran.

Blake finally exhaled heavily over my denying him a third time and climbed off me and my bed.

I sucked air into my lungs, focusing on getting them gone so I could return to Mom and real life. My night of freedom had ended with the rising sun. It was time to focus on reality.

Chapter 14

Blake

Third time's a charm.

Utter fucking bullshit.

Wren had turned me down as though the passion that had unleashed the night before, the way our mouths had sent her soaring that morning, hadn't meant a damn thing.

She'd asked for a one-and-done hookup by text, but I felt sure once she had a taste of the pleasure I could give her she would want more.

I made the most pathetic walk of shame down her stairs in front of Reid, without the offer of coffee, without any hope of seeing her again.

I didn't know what the fuck to say or think. Wren had blown my mind, surprising me with her intensity. Even though our gazes hadn't held while I'd sunk into her body over and over again, the stirrings of connection between us had only grown stronger. Every cry from her lips, every moan we'd worked from her chest had marked my soul like a hot poker's brand.

She didn't want me—but she fucking *owned* me.

Once would never be enough.

I rarely lingered beyond the first fuck, and Reid and I bracketing a woman we'd pleasured as she passed out without even discussing it? It hadn't ever happened. But Reid had seemed to know what I'd wanted and had climbed in on her other side without comment.

"Fuck." I slammed my car door and grasped my steering wheel.

Reid eyed me from the passenger seat.

"Fuck!" I hollered again.

"Blake."

"Goddamnit!"

"Talk to me, brother," he murmured.

I started the truck and backed out onto the street, jaw working. "What the fuck am I doing *wrong?*" I asked through clenched teeth.

He had to have felt the tension between Wren and I when he'd exited the bathroom to find me yanking my clothes on.

She'd slipped off the bed and quickly wrapped herself in a robe as though donning armor to keep me firmly fixed *out* of her life.

One word had slashed at my chest, knifed through my heart.

My throat had swelled while shoving my shoes back on and making for the front door.

Thankfully, Reid had scurried to dress and followed me out into the hot, muggy morning.

Not even seven, and the moisture could be wrung from the air.

I flicked on my AC full blast and sped toward the highway.

"She didn't even give me a chance to ask her out again,"

I muttered, adrenaline still coursing through my blood. "I simply said her name." Same as the morning at the foot of her stairs when she'd collapsed into me as though relieved I'd offered myself to her. A muscle ticked in my jaw. "That's it. Got a firm *no* that fucking hurt like hell."

Reid didn't speak, which was for the best. Chances were, he had a ton of shit to tease me with on his tongue, but he bit it back, knowing I wasn't in the fucking mood.

We drove southward on Route 95, trees flashing by as the sun filtered through them on our right. A new morning. A new beginning.

I'd hoped Wren's giving in to me physically had meant the start of something we could build upon, the promise of more I hadn't realized how badly I'd set my sights on.

I rubbed a hand over my face, slumping in my seat and propping my wrist atop the steering wheel.

"Thank fuck I didn't kiss her," I muttered. I couldn't even imagine how the dismissal, the rejection, would have felt had I devoured her mouth like I'd longed to do.

We'd shared a deep intimacy through our bodies but had kept our souls from entwining too.

Reid had gotten a taste.

I glanced over to find his gaze fixed on me. "Did she kiss you back?"

"You know she did."

"No." I returned my attention back on the road. "I mean, did she like...initiate it?"

"Yes."

Fuck.

I swallowed hard. "She didn't even try with me."

"You didn't give her a chance."

"I did." I'd been a handspan away from her mouth, losing myself in her hazel-brown eyes still heavy-lidded from the release we'd given her. I hadn't just been gazing down at her readying myself to ask for a chance but for permission to take too.

She'd heard my thoughts. I could see it in her eyes.

"She turned away from me," I told Reid, hating the memory of her thinned lips as though the thought of moving them over mine sickened her.

I was good enough to fuck, but that was it.

"Are you going to give me a black eye?" Reid asked.

I snorted. "I'm envious as fuck, not a jealous prick."

"But you could be over her." Reid knew me too damn well. "There's no hiding you're possessive of her, so you fucking blew my mind by turning her toward me, all but telling me to keep her mouth occupied."

"If I get one taste..." I shook my head. "It's like my instincts were trying to keep me from being denied a third time."

Reid squeezed my shoulder. "She's got a lot going on right now."

He spoke truth, but she'd been pretty clear her mind had been made up about me. Fucking judgment. Not even giving me a chance to show her I was more than what the world saw...what I hadn't let anyone see after Sara back in high school.

If anyone wouldn't care, it would be Reid. At least I hoped.

"I love Star Trek," I blurted.

"What?" Reid asked, his voice high—half laughing.

My insides tightened at the thought he would make fun of me too and decide I was too much of a geek to hang with.

"I've been a Trekkie since middle school," I barely managed to strangle out the words of my secret but felt I needed to. "The first time I saw Deanna Troi, I was done for, head over heels in love."

"Holy shit." Reid chuckled. "Add a hint of green to her eyes, and Wren would look just like her."

My head whipped his way, my eyes wide as fuck. "What? You know who I'm talking about?"

"You aren't the only closet nerd in this truck," he said with a chuckle.

"Oh my fucking God." I barked a laugh, all the tension and expectation of rejection draining out of me. "Are you serious right now?"

"I always preferred Tasha," Reid said.

Yeah, he'd been a sucker for blondes since I'd known him.

"Why have you hidden that part of you from me?" I asked.

"Why'd you do it to me?" Reid shot back.

We grinned at each other, and he punched my shoulder as I faced forward once more.

"Star Wars fan?" Reid asked.

"Fuck yeah."

"Lord of the Rings?"

"Definitely," I admitted, loving how free I felt over admitting my silly insecurities.

"Same, brother." Reid snickered.

"That's why Sara broke up with me in high school, you know," I admitted what I'd lied about all those years ago. "My sister told her we were going to Comic Con in Boston and that I always dressed up like Boba Fett. Sara made fun of me, but at least it was in the privacy of our home and not in front of the football team or something."

Reid outright laughed. "Why the fuck didn't we bond

over this shit as kids? I figured you would think I was imma-ture or some shit."

"Same." I shot him another grin.

"So what are you going to do about Wren?" he asked when I'd rather have bullshitted over our favorite episodes and shows to keep my brain occupied.

My chest went heavy again. "What can I do? She's got her hands full with her mom—at least...fuck." I hit my steering wheel. "I didn't even fucking ask her how her mom was doing! Is it any fucking wonder she hates me? I show up, and you share more words with her than I do because I'm tongue-tied, and all I can think about is getting inside her body."

"That's what she invited us over for, Blake," Reid said, his tone low and calm. "Her eyes were troubled but also shut off. She wasn't interested in any questions or deep discussions. She wanted to forget for a while."

"Shit." I blew out an exhale. "Do you think her mom passed and she wanted to keep from grieving?"

"Could be."

"Jesus Christ, I'm a selfish prick."

Reid didn't refute my harshly spewed statement. "What are you going to do?"

"I'll text once I'm home."

We rode in mostly silence the rest of the way, and I dropped Reid off at his apartment.

"See you tomorrow," he said, climbing from my truck. "And let me know how it goes with Wren if she'll talk to you."

I nodded.

A whole fucking Sunday ahead of me with nothing to do.

I'd woken earlier than Wren that morning and had

watched her sleep, daydreaming about spending the day with her. Sending Reid home in my truck so I could shower with her. Going to grab Dunks together in her piece-of-shit car. Maybe sitting beside the river and getting to know each other better.

Disappointment had never tasted so bitter.

I got to my condo and sprawled on the couch, cell in hand to text Wren.

Me: **I'm an ass for not asking about your mom.**

I chewed on the inside of my lip while waiting for an answer. Eventually, I grew aggravated at the silence as minutes slid passed.

If she had to go to her mom's, it was possible she was still on the road.

Hopping in the shower gave me something to do, but I hated washing the scent of her off my skin knowing full well she'd never offer me another opportunity to touch or taste her again.

A long text waited for me when I finally made my way back out to the living room, a cup of coffee in hand.

Little Bird: **She's near the end but still hanging on. Thank you for helping me forget last night. You and Reid were a great distraction. I'm sorry for being so blunt and mean this morning, but I can't think beyond my full plate. I hope you can understand.**

What sucked is that I could. Thoroughly.

But her words had brought a tingle of hope to thread back through my heart, stitching up the tears her coldness had created.

My fingers shook as I texted back.

Me: **I'm only a phone call or text away if you need anything.**

A million other words wanted to spill from my mind into cyberspace, but I tucked them away. I wished her mom's suffering would stop but didn't want to state I hoped she died. I longed for Wren's sorrow to be short, but that too meant I wanted her mom gone sooner than later.

Wren: **Thank you.**

Setting aside my phone, I focused on my coffee, fingers crossed she would remember me in her time of need.

Chapter 15

Wren

Reid was hot and all, but it was the memory of Blake's hands, his tongue on me that I couldn't rid from my mind.

I'd never known such release, the utter bliss like they'd given me, and I felt like shit over how I'd kicked the men to the curb. They'd been nothing but selfless while loving on my body after waking up.

Immersing myself in classwork Sunday afternoon, I'd managed to forget about Blake for a few moments at a time but found myself staring out Mom's apartment window overlooking a busy street. Lost in fantasies of what could never be.

Somehow, I managed to sleep Sunday night without his navy blue eyes and talented tongue on my pussy haunting my dreams.

Mom claimed she was fine on her own while I went to class on Monday. When I got home, I tackled cleaning out the old linen closet in the hallway while she napped.

Again with the damn wayward thoughts about Blake.

How many blonde women had he teased with his hands

and mouth? How many had he enticed onto his dick? How many holes had he plundered while chasing his own release?

Ugh.

I hated that I would judge him for having an active sex life. What the hell did it matter to me? Why did I even care?

Jealousy.

The word whispered through my head.

"No. Nope." I pressed my lips tight. No fucking way was it green envy stirring shit up in my mind.

I glared at the tattered set of sheets I held in my hands, hating how I lied to myself. They were older than me and smelled of smoke and slight mildew, worth only taking up space in the trash.

"Wren."

Mom's croak pulled me away from the shit between my ears, and I ambled into her room to find her more awake than she'd been for weeks.

Eyes clear, she stared at me as I moved through the remaining clutter in her room.

I'd stopped asking how she felt days earlier, when she'd bitten my head off and reminded me her insides were shit.

"Are you hungry? Thirsty?" I asked, and she shook her head.

"Sit."

Taking up my usual spot in the threadbare recliner beside her bed, I studied her face. Even more gaunt and skeletal, she appeared to be at death's door. I hated my conflicting emotions of wanting her suffering to end but not being ready to say goodbye just yet.

"It's time for me to confess my sins," she murmured, her voice thin and weak.

I patted her bony hand where it lay listless atop the comforter but didn't entwine my fingers with hers since she didn't like affection. "I'm not a priest, Mom."

"Don't need a damn priest since my sins aren't against him." Her watery eyes caressed over my face as though getting one last good look.

My throat grew tight. "It's okay, Mom. You don't have to tell me anything."

"Need to even though it's selfish as fuck." She closed her eyes and straightened her head to rest on her thin pillow. "I did my best by you."

"I know, Mom," I whispered, hating how I still ached for hugs and kisses I'd never gotten.

"You came screaming into the world and changed my life forever."

I laughed lightly, tears welling in my eyes. My noisiness had always driven her nuts. Once I'd hit middle school and puberty though, I'd become self-conscious. Quieter. Shy.

We'd gotten along much better after that.

"I couldn't pay the bills even before you came along," Mom said, her voice reedy, and she struggled to fill her lungs.

She'd been a product of the system, barely managing to scrape by once she became of age, something I'd also known.

"I did whatever necessary to make a living before getting pregnant with you."

Those were words I'd never heard her speak before, and my eyebrows downturned, unease rising up inside me.

"But I got desperate," she whispered.

I guessed where she headed and wanted to steer her off the path of confession I had no wish to hear. "It's okay, Mom. You don't have to—"

"I lied to you about your father."

Stilling, I watched as she tried to swallow, my own heart in my throat.

"He wasn't the love of my life," she whispered. "He was just some john whose condom broke."

My breath left like I'd been punched in the chest, leaving me sagging in the chair.

"I-I didn't want you knowing you were the product of... well, not that a story your daddy took off on us was any better. But I can't go to the grave without telling you the truth, Wren. I just can't..." A heavy sigh shuddered through her, and I struggled to keep my chin from trembling.

Mom had resorted to prostitution to make a living.

And some no-name, faceless dude paid her to find release into a condom.

That broke.

Just fucking lovely.

"I—I felt shame for what I did, but decided to make it up to you. I don't know shit about love and affection, but I tried to provide for the life I'd given you. But it wore on me. Was too much, and...and I gave in to things that pulled me down."

Drugs.

"Did you tell him?" I asked, my voice barely above a ragged whisper.

"I never saw him other than that one time."

I couldn't even ask how she knew for sure who had fathered me if she'd been selling her body regularly.

She hadn't lied about his first name she'd shared with me years ago, the made-up love of her life who'd left her brokenhearted and pregnant.

John.

Closing my eyes, I swallowed down tears.

Talk about a damn identity crisis. Who the hell needed one of those on top of the other shit I faced?

"You're right, Mom," I whispered, my voice ragged. "That *was* a selfish confession."

I got up and walked out, too damn broken inside to feel any empathy or offer understanding for why she'd hidden the truth from me.

My mother, the prostitute.

My father, an unknown man who'd paid her for sex.

Maybe that was why she hadn't ever been affectionate with me—she'd never wanted me. Hadn't loved me.

I stared at the closet I'd been cleaning out, feeling so damn empty. Lost. I'd thought of myself as white trash before, but holy fucking hell.

Shame and embarrassment flooded through me, heating my face and making my body desire to sink into the ground.

I was nothing more than an oops, unplanned and definitely unwanted.

Mom should have given me up for adoption. Allowed me a chance to have a family take me in that could afford to feed and clothe me without selling their bodies.

I'd been the burden that had sent her spiraling into addiction.

"Fucking hell," I muttered, tipping my head back to stare at the stained ceiling as tears ran down my cheeks.

I'd worked so damn hard to escape where I'd come from, but I realized in that moment, my beginning could never be changed. I might rise above my circumstances, but my soul was stained by sins that would never be scrubbed clean.

𝕱𝕬

I didn't share the truth with Jenny who was pretty much my only friend. It was bad enough I often felt her eyes on me whenever we worked the night shift together. She pitied my circumstances, the looming death of my mom, and how I struggled to meet deadlines for my summer course.

At least that part ended on Friday with my final test, but I couldn't seem to rouse any excitement due to the shit I'd learned a few days prior. I hadn't spoken a word to my mom outside medically necessary shit since.

"I'm taking you out Friday night," Jenny said, her tone firm. "We're going to celebrate your damn summer class ending."

"I'm not really in the mood," I muttered, pouring small white tablets into the pill counter.

"Too bad. You need some distraction, a little *you* time."

I hadn't told her about my first threesome the weekend before where I'd found exactly what she wanted to give me. It was the confession Mom had slammed upside my head that had brought me too low to even think about much else.

There were hours my focus remained on how my life came to be rather than on Blake who I thought I'd never rid my mind of.

Bottling up the prescription, I considered Jenny's offer.

I did need something—and no way would I text Blake for another booty call.

He hadn't been too put off to fuck me by the fact I'd grown up dirt-poor in the City of Sin, but if he found out the rest...

Well, that was one sure way to keep him from asking me out for a fourth time at least.

He'd checked in with me throughout the week, asking about Mom, but I hadn't replied beyond a simple **Still breathing**.

"So."

I turned toward Jenny who studied the computer screen as she entered in a called-in prescription for someone heading in from the ER.

"Friday night. You, me. Some drinks, dinner…oh! What about Encore?"

I hadn't been to the casino in Everett since I pinched every penny I earned. "I'm not into gambling."

"You don't have to spend a dime. I'll wine and dine you then we can just mosey around and watch others drain their bank accounts. What do you say?"

I couldn't deny being curious about seeing the inside of the new casino. "Fine."

She laughed. "Don't sound so excited."

I shrugged.

"See, this is why you need a night on the town. I'll make it one you'll never forget."

"I feel like I'm taking advantage of Nancy," I muttered, even though we were able to keep a baby monitor beside Mom so Nancy could sleep on the other side of the wall in her own apartment rather than spending the night on my old mattress when I worked.

"From what you've said, she's more than happy to help. Paying it forward or whatever."

"Yeah." I shrugged and retrieved another bottle off the shelf to fill the pain medication prescribed for one of our usual customers.

"So don't let yourself feel guilty. You should be selfish for a change."

Selfish.

As if I needed the reminder of how I didn't want to be like my mom.

But Jenny was right. Nancy didn't mind. In fact, she'd

already encouraged me to take one night that weekend for myself.

"Okay. Friday. Encore but no gambling."

"Yes!" Jenny actually fist-bumped the air like she'd scored a goal or something.

I huffed a laugh. "Thank you for caring about my sorry ass."

"There's nothing sorry about your ass," she countered with a waggle of her eyebrows. "It's tiny and cute. Maybe we'll find some sugar daddy to fuck your worries away for a couple of hours."

I fought to keep my small smile in place as it wanted to turn into a grimace. *That* I had zero interest in.

Blake

I didn't want to bother Wren. Fuck knew what she dealt with from day to day. Twice during the week I'd texted to check in with her, and I'd gotten short answers letting me know her mother was still alive.

The guys at work avoided me, and even Reid couldn't handle my miserable ass for more than a few minutes at a time.

I'd never been so damn off my game, almost unhinged in how I pined for Wren.

But it was the desire to wrap her up in my arms in order to comfort not just find release.

My cell pinged, and I swiped it off my desk.

Micah: **I've got a favor to ask.**

He already still owed me for the two original favors for hanging with the Renshaws while they'd fucked. I'd sat in with them two weeks earlier and was surprised they hadn't asked for me since.

Me: **Renshaws?**

I asked for clarity, not really even sure I wanted to watch them go at it again. I already struggled with my mind's fixation on Wren and didn't need the sight of that woman lavishing love on her husband when I yearned for the same thing.

Micah: **Eye candy.**

Memories from the Saturday before flitted through my brain. That boring-as-fuck event that had ended up being a complete a waste of my evening.

At least the night had ended with some of the best sex of my life.

Micah's next text came in before I could hit reply. **But nothing like last time**.

Me: **I planned to get trashed with Reid so I can stop thinking about Wren.**

He'd heard through the grapevine about our hookup and my broken heart. Reid didn't know how to keep his mouth shut.

Micah: **Go out with Jarod instead. I'll make it worth your while.**

I snorted. **Promises, promises**, I replied.

Micah: **Seriously, man, it's a last minute thing for my cousin.**

Me: **No one else is available?**

Micah: **She requested hot and hunky.**

A laugh ripped from my chest. **I can see why you called me first.**

Micah: **Anyone ever tell you you're an arrogant asshole?**

I huffed. **Plenty**, I shot back.

Micah: **All you have to do is hang with a couple of ladies living it up at Encore tonight. Get their drinks. Watch their backs. Maybe**

dance if they want. But Jenny told me they aren't exactly looking for sex.

Which meant they weren't *not* looking to get laid either.

My dick isn't for hire, I reminded him.

Micah: **I mentioned that you were my only option since the rest of my guys were booked. Jarod's presence is already costing me an extra couple hundred—out of my own damn pocket.**

Micah must really love his cousin.

Me: **Are you giving us spending cash and am I allowed to have alcohol at least?**

Micah: **I *do* owe you…**

"Why not," I muttered, texting back an affirmative, stating I'd gladly enjoy some expensive whiskey on his dime and gamble away a little of his money.

Since it was for his cousin and I still wasn't officially on his payroll, he told me he wouldn't need me to sign any contract. He also informed me Jarod would pick me up for the evening and have an envelope of cash to ensure I didn't regret helping him out.

Hopefully, the women spoke English and weren't complete bores to the point I craved more than two drinks.

⅏

Jarod showed up in his old BMW, dressed in black jeans and a sharp olive-green button-down, the sleeves rolled up to show off his vein-covered forearms.

"Easy night tonight," he said as I buckled in. He handed over the promised cash from Micah. "Don't know how you talked him into that." Jarod nodded toward the envelope in my hand and pulled out into traffic.

"Fucker owes me."

"So what—are you an actual employee now or just the guy in Micah's back pocket when he's desperate?"

"This is my last time," I told Jarod what I hadn't even shared with Micah.

"How come?"

"My heart is set on this sweet little woman, and even though she doesn't want me, it just doesn't feel right getting paid by Elite Escorts."

"If you're not together, what's the problem with accepting money to keep other women company or having your voyeur kink fulfilled?" Jarod asked, glancing in his side mirror before switching lanes. "It's not like you're a dick for hire with that girl waiting on you at home, none the wiser."

Wren had already judged me for having a different woman every night—which I hadn't had anyone else at *all* since meeting her. I expected she would hate me even more if she found out an escort company had paid me decent money over the previous couple of weeks just to watch others fuck and act as eye candy for people who had too much cash and didn't know how to get actual dates.

The thought curdled my dinner in my stomach, and I turned my focus toward the night ahead.

"So what's the plan?" I asked.

"His cousin somehow landed tickets to a show at the Mémoire Nightclub, but we're meeting them at the Center Bar."

I'd been to the casino a few times and nodded, glad to hear we wouldn't just be following drunk women around the casino floor while they lost all their money. "So, no gambling?"

Jarod shrugged and exited off Route 1 into Everett. "Don't know, don't care. We just gotta look good and keep their drinks filled until they're ready for Ricky to pick them up."

Ricky was the Elite Escorts' main driver and was usually reserved for the bigwigs who used Micah's services.

"He's sending the limo?" I asked.

"It's his cousin, man. There's nothing he won't do for family. Besides, there weren't any other clients tonight who'd requested transportation."

"Any idea who the woman is?"

"Her name is Jenny, and she's blonde like Micah—that's all I was told. Here." Jarod fished his cell from his pocket and handed it over after using Face ID to unlock the screen. "Micah's last text."

I clicked it open to find a pretty woman who looked like the female version of my friend. "She's hot and at least she speaks English," I muttered, strangely unmoved by the sight of the woman that would have gotten my blood going before I'd met Wren.

Jarod barked a laugh. "Yeah, there's that."

I handed the cell back to him.

Since the valet service was free, Jarod pulled up to the main entrance and handed his keys over.

A few minutes later, we strode into the casino. The place was busier than the last few times I'd gone to hang with a couple of the guys from work, but we had no problems weaving our way toward the agreed upon meeting spot.

It was a little after eight-thirty, and no one looking like the contact approached us before we reached Center Bar.

"Want a drink while we wait?" Jarod asked.

"The most expensive whiskey they've got on the rocks."

He chuckled and flagged down a bartender.

I turned and scanned the crowd for the blonde—Jenny.

Jarod handed me my drink before I could spot Micah's cousin. "Thanks."

"You can thank Micah later."

We clinked our glasses together and sipped.

"So tell me about this woman who has your panties all twisted up," Jarod said.

"I'd rather talk about your job as a nurse," I muttered. "Trying to keep my mind off her."

"Sorry—and yeah, I get that." Jarod glanced around the room, and I did the same. "I work at MGfC's Pediatric Leukemia Clinic."

"Shit, man. How the fuck do you do that?" I couldn't imagine seeing sick and dying kids every day.

"I had leukemia when I was a kid," Jarod said with a shrug as though it was no big deal. "There were a couple amazing nurses who took care of me, and I decided if I beat the odds, I would be there for other little ones who suffered like I did."

"Goddamn." I shook my head, in absolute awe of the man. No way in fuck could I work in a clinic like that.

"There she is." Jarod nodded with his chin toward the casino's entrance.

I caught sight of the female Micah look-alike weaving through the crowd, but it was the shorter woman walking beside her that stole my breath.

"Oh fuck." I swallowed hard.

"What?" Jarod asked.

"That's her—that's Wren."

Jarod chuckled and finished off his whiskey in one swallow. "Looks like fate decided to give you a little luck for a change." He clasped my shoulder and started toward the two women who hadn't yet caught sight of us.

Fate.

In that moment, I hated the bitch—because Wren was about to find out what I did when bored and caved to Micah's begging.

I stood like a damn deer in the headlights, my chest caving in and my lungs seizing.

I'm officially fucked.

Chapter 17

Wren

The Tik Tok Chicken Jenny and I had shared at Mystique had hit the spot but didn't do much to soak up the apricot sangria I'd sucked down while waiting for our meal.

I hadn't gone to a restaurant in...months. Not since my last date earlier in the year. January? Or was it February when my ex had broken up with me? Whenever it was, I'd been set against any man messing with my school mojo until long after I graduated and landed a good paying job.

Jenny had been right though.

I needed a girl's night out where I didn't have to worry about getting home early or drinking too much. Mom had seemed stable and Nancy sat with her, so I didn't feel guilty taking some time to myself.

The final earlier that morning had been a hell of a lot easier than I'd expected, and I'd gone home and conked out, finally sleeping until I felt fully rested.

We'd taken the T into the casino, but Jenny told me she already had a ride to get us home whenever we were ready to call it a night.

She kept checking her cell as though anxious to get to the casino. The show she'd bought tickets for didn't start until nine, but I figured she wanted to arrive early.

"Come on," she said, grabbing my elbow to get me walking faster through the hallway.

"What's the rush?" I asked, stumbling in the heels she had insisted I wear with the only black cocktail dress I owned.

"I have a surprise." She sounded giddy, and I glanced up to find her head swiveling as we entered the casino, her long blonde hair in natural waves flowing over her perfect cleavage.

"What?"

"You'll see in a minute."

She dragged me toward a double stairway leading to the second floor that overlooked the one we crossed.

"Oh my God! There he is," she squealed.

"Who?"

"Jarod."

I couldn't see over the taller people in front of me, but my stomach took a sudden lurch over whatever little surprise she'd set up.

"Who's Jarod?" I asked, wariness heightening my voice.

"One of our two dates for the night."

Dates.

"I thought we were having a girl's night out," I muttered, sidestepping a hulking guy in front of me to follow on Jenny's heels, thinking it might be smarter to turn around and run away.

"We did—and now we can enjoy some male company thanks to my cousin Micah..." Jenny's voice trailed off, her steps slowing. "Oh. My. God."

"What?" I stumbled to a stop beside her, following her line of sight.

A dark-haired cutie approached us, a grin on his face, but it was the man beyond his shoulder who stared me down, his eyes on the verge of bugging out.

"Blake." I gasped his name.

"Isn't that..."

"Yeah," I whispered.

"Blake Harper is one of Micah's Elite Escorts?" Jenny asked, her tone giddy as hell.

I blinked. Whipped my head toward my friend to find her grinning like a fool.

"What are the chances?" She giggled.

"Escorts...as in paid *escorts*, escorts?" I asked, sure I'd heard wrong, my stomach churning.

"Male prostitutes to put it bluntly, but yeah. My cousin hooked us up—and damn did he ever. I'm guessing you'll want Blake. I'll take Jarod."

My stomach flipped, and I swallowed hard.

Blake Harper.

Paid escort.

Prostitute.

Like someone pulled the trigger on my vomit reflex, I heaved, barely managing to keep my dinner from spewing past my lips by quickly swallowing a few times.

My ears rang as I caught Blake's gaze through the mingling crowd between us.

The look of fear—regret—in his eyes was like the cocking of the shotgun that held my emotions in check.

"I-I have to go," I whispered.

"What?" Jenny grabbed my arm again before I could spin away. "Why? What's wrong?"

"I have to go," I repeated, my legs starting to shake. "I-I can't do this."

"It's okay, really! Micah gifted me the two guys for the night to just hang out. They're our drink fetchers and whatever else we desire. You don't have to sleep with Blake—unless you want to."

I'd already allowed him to fuck me.

He's a male prostitute.

"I'm going to be sick." But I stood rooted as though vines had reached through the casino floor and wrapped up around my ankles.

Jarod reached us first, his exchanging names with Jenny barely reaching through the fog growing between my ears. Blake swallowed hard and started toward us, his focus glued to my face.

My knees locked up to keep me from falling over, and my pulse sputtered as though the engine of my heart stalled.

I'd all but accused Blake of being a whore that first time he'd asked me out. How right I'd been. He was worse than a playboy, sticking his dick into blonde bimbos—for money.

Was he hooked on drugs too like Mom? Had he gotten into financial trouble and needed the cash? He certainly didn't look or act like an addict.

Maybe he just wanted easy pussy.

Maybe that was why he'd been so damn set on getting me to go out with him—the challenge. He never got turned down.

Hell, he got *paid* to have sex with women.

Heat flared to life in my guts, overshadowing the roiling nausea. How many babies had he unknowingly spawned through faulty condoms?

Lips tight and chin lifted, I narrowed my gaze at him, clutching my small purse in a death grip at my side.

His gaze flicked over to Jenny as he drew closer, his charming smile fake as shit, his hand trembling as he reached out to shake hers.

"Blake Harper," he said, his voice thin and almost... nervous rather than filled with his usual confidence.

"Jenny Fox," my friend said. "And this is Wren."

Both men turned toward me, but I kept my stare on Blake's wary face.

"Why am I not surprised?" I somehow managed to snip my words, clueing him in to how pissed I was.

"Wren?" Jenny asked, confusion lacing her tone.

"I assumed you were a whore, but seriously?"

Blake's face flushed. "Wren—"

"Don't bother, Blake." I shook my head, realizing I'd gained full control over my body again. "Don't *even* bother." I pivoted on my heels to face Jenny, dismissing the two men entirely. "I'm sorry to run out on you like this, but I need to leave. Enjoy your two...*escorts*. I'm sure they'll willingly rock your world if you're up for a threesome."

My legs trembled, but I managed to stalk away without tripping and falling on my face.

"Wren!" Jenny called after me, but it was a firm, masculine grip that caught my elbow halfway across the casino floor.

I yanked from Blake's hold and continued on as though he didn't exist.

"Wren, wait. Please." He hurried to get directly into my path, and I stopped, tipping my head back to meet his gaze as he loomed over me.

A slew of emotions ran over his face, vulnerability being the most laughable.

"Do you take acting classes too, Blake?" I asked, my face

hot, my entire body jittery from embarrassment, anger, and his nearness, which I told myself I loathed.

"What? No! I can explain."

"I don't need an explanation," I stated firmly through gritted teeth. "I was right about the red flags waving in my head about you. Thank *fuck* I hadn't given into your supposed charms. Those puppy dog eyes. You begging me for a date like the mere sight of me had lit you up from the inside out."

All trace of arrogance had fled the building, and I wanted to clap at his performance of being horrified and heartbroken over his little secret leaking out to a woman he'd supposedly crushed on.

"You couldn't stand the fact a woman would tell you no." I shook my head, disgust curling my lips. "And now I know why."

"I'm not a whore," Blake whisper-hollered, leaning down nearer my face.

I snorted and moved around him, once more focused on exiting the building.

"I'm not!"

"And Elite Escorts isn't a get-dick-for-cash service?" I shot back, my strides quick to keep him from getting in front of me again and impeding my race to escape the building.

"Wren, let me explain!" he repeated. "Please!"

I spun to face him, my arms flying. "I don't care!" I shrieked, drawing all sorts of attention, but I couldn't find two fucks to give if people knew who—*what*—the senator's grandson really was. "It doesn't matter to me who you fuck or how much money you get paid for it!"

"Then why are you hollering?"

"Because you—my mom—fuck!" My eyes hazed over as a sob rose inside my chest.

Nope. Nuh uh.

"Leave. Me. Alone." I took off once more, fumbling to get my cell out of my purse.

Uber, I mouthed to myself, my hands shaking like crazy.

I stepped outside into the night air as tears tracked down my cheeks. Careless of the mascara that had to be running like a river, I approached the nearest valet and begged him to help me find a ride home.

Blake, for once, did the smart thing.

He accepted the fact I wanted nothing to do with his ass.

Chapter 18

Blake

God fucking damnit.

I stood inside the glass doors, watching Wren talk to one of the valet attendants. The guy held her shoulders, and I seethed over the fact she would allow an absolute stranger to offer her comfort as she cried.

Running my hands through my hair, I stared after her. My feet stuck unmoving when I wanted to rush out there and demand she listen to my side of the story before judging me *yet again.*

She'd thoroughly flipped out as though I'd betrayed her in some way, and I'd never felt so shitty, so...dirty.

A jagged knife twisted in my chest, serrated edges ripping at flesh and bone. Agony ate at the wound, leaving me with a sense of hopelessness I couldn't handle.

Blake Harper, rich pretty boy, playboy bachelor who grew up with a silver spoon in his mouth, devastated by the most stunning, fiery woman he'd ever met.

The only one to ever catch my eye and steal a piece of me I didn't even know I had inside.

Desire for something more. Real.

And I'd somehow fucked shit up even worse than the weekend before.

"Fuck." I ripped at my hair, flinching when Jarod clasped my shoulder.

"The fuck, man?"

"I...we." My jaw clenched.

Jenny stood on my other side. "What the hell did you do to her, Blake?"

Begged her to go out with me three times.

Shared her with my best friend because it was the only way to get a taste of her.

And I hadn't guarded my heart.

"I fell hard and fast," I whispered. "Then I fucked up."

"What did you do?" Jenny pushed again, and I turned my focus on her.

"I...I don't know. But I'm not really an escort," I rushed to explain, hoping she would at least listen and tell Wren. "I don't get paid for sex. Micah is a good friend and was in a bind so I agreed to hang out with you guys tonight. I swear."

"He's telling the truth," Jarod input. "Blake isn't an actual employee. He's not a prostitute."

Jenny let out a huff and pushed through the doors as though I hadn't said a word, leaving me and Jarod alone. She went right up to Wren and wrapped her arms around her smaller friend.

"Want another whiskey?" Jarod asked, and I nodded, tearing my gaze off the woman who'd brought me lower than I'd ever imagined.

"Yeah. Maybe three or four."

Jarod clasped my shoulder and led me back the way we'd come. "I'm all ears."

So I told him about the previous couple of months from start to finish, leaving nothing out.

"There's got to be more to the story," he said when I finished.

I'd slammed back three shots and lusted for the buzz to kick my ass into numbness. "That's it."

We managed to snag a couple bar chairs at the second floor sports bar for me to drink my sorrows away. Jarod nursed a beer while I lifted my empty shot glass at the closest bartender.

"It doesn't make sense," Jarod said.

"She's judged me from day one—hell, before she even met me, Wren decided I was nothing more than a player out to get some since that's what my social media portrays."

"But you're not?"

I opened my mouth to refute the fact but realized I couldn't.

That was the pre-Wren Blake. She'd changed me the moment I'd laid eyes on her. Not love at first sight. I didn't believe in that shit. Definitely lust but...more.

I rubbed at my aching chest before downing the whiskey poured into my glass.

"You might want to take it easy."

Snorting, I shook my head.

"*Take it easy,*" Jarod changed his wording and tone. "I'm not allowing your drunk ass in my car. You know how hard it is to get the stench of vomit out of carpet?"

I heaved a sigh, my hazed eyesight on the huge screen above us. I had no fucking clue what sport it was. Couldn't focus. Didn't care.

"She thinks I'm scum." Yeah, maybe my words slurred a little.

"Because she doesn't know you."

"And now my chances of changing that have shit the bed. Fuck." I ran my hands through my hair again.

"Come on, big guy. Let's get you home." Jarod slapped a few bills on the bar and stood, grabbing my elbow.

I slid from the chair and suddenly realized how much I'd drank. "Oh shit."

"Yeah." Jarod wound his arm around my waist, and I leaned into him.

"Not gay," I stated firmly. Or I tried to at least. My tongue felt swollen as fuck.

"Neither am I, but your ass isn't making it downstairs without help."

"You're right." I nodded, leaning into my newest best friend. "What would you do if me were you?"

Jarod laughed. "What?"

"You were me?"

"You're drunk."

"Yep."

"I would give her time to calm down," Jarod said we hit the stairs to head to the first floor. "Then I'd send her a long-as-fuck text explaining the situation. Give her Micah's number if that's the proof she wants. Hell, have Micah reach out to her. He owes you, doesn't he?"

"Fuck yeah, he does," I muttered, thinking I was ready to crash on my bed and not move for a few days.

Saturday.

I could sleep in tomorrow.

I grinned until I realized that meant no work, just empty hours with nothing to do but feel sorry for myself. I would dream about the little birdie who had taken me down so many damn notches I floundered in the sewer drains of what had once been a pretty damn good life.

My stomach churned at the thought.

"Oh fuck." I swallowed hard.

"You gonna be sick?"

"Mmm."

Jarod detoured for the closest bathroom, and I managed to hold back spewing until I fell to my knees in front of the porcelain throne.

JE

I didn't want to give Wren the two days Jarod suggested.

Sunday afternoon, I continued to wallow and decided I'd waited long enough. Since I couldn't emphasize or use any tone of voice to inflict emotion into my explanation, I fought to find the right words that wouldn't make me sound like a bored rich guy who had nothing better to do than play pretend escort for one of his closest friends.

With her prejudice, she would assume that regardless of my verbiage.

But she wouldn't answer if I called, and I would stumble around like an idiot if I attempted to leave a message.

Huffing a cleansing exhale that did nothing to steady my nerves, I grabbed my cell off my coffee table where it had been silently mocking me for a solid sixty minutes while I'd grappled over words she might actually read and believe.

My phone pinged in my hands, and I flinched.

Wren.

"No fucking way." I swiped the screen to life, muttering for the damn thing to read my face faster so I could get to her long-as-fuck text.

Wren: **Jenny told me what you said, and I'm sorry for not allowing you the opportunity to explain.**

My breath left in a rush, and I continued reading, sagging back against the couch.

I hate to unload even more shit about my past, but it will explain my reaction to Jenny's surprise of hiring two escorts for the rest of our night. I found out last Sunday that my mom sold herself on the streets to keep a roof over her head. She also confessed the truth that my father hadn't been her knight in shining armor, the one true love she'd always claimed him to be.

The sperm donor had been a john who'd worn a faulty condom.

So that's the story of how I spawned to life, Blake.

I'm nothing more than white trash. A prostitute's daughter, the offspring of a drug addict. Yes, she did everything she could to feed and house me, but I probably would have been better off if she'd given me up for adoption.

I scrubbed a hand down over my face, that damn knife sliding into my chest again but for a different reason. "Holy fucking shit," I muttered, shaking my head.

While I don't condemn people for doing what they have to in order to survive, I couldn't stomach the thought of someone as blessed as you selling yourself like my mom did. Prostitution led her into addiction. Abusing various drugs ruined her body and has slowly been shutting down her internal organs at too young of an age.

Watching her slowly wither away into bones and skin has not been easy, nor pleasant. I wouldn't wish this on any child, regardless of their relationship with their parent.

I hope you can understand and maybe even forgive me for being such a self-righteous bitch in the heat of the moment.

If you're still wondering, yes, my mom still breathing, but she slipped into unconsciousness last night while I was out with Jenny. That is yet another sliver of guilt I'll have tacked onto my brain for the times I'm feeling bad about myself. I was out living it up and enjoying myself while Mom's final hours took her responses, reactions, and words away from me forever.

My throat went tight as fuck, and I blinked the haze to finish reading Wren's text.

Your little notes have seen me through many of my down hours, and the trinkets lining my bookshelves bring small smiles whenever I stop by my apartment to water my plants. I'm guessing I'll be back there before the end of the week since Mom's time is incredibly short.

Anyway, thank you for your encouragement, and again, I'm sorry.

I tipped my head back and closed my eyes, my hands limp on my lap, the cell sliding onto the cushion beside me. Jesus fucking Christ that poor woman—both of them.

Wren had told me her mom had no one growing up,

that she'd been dirt-poor and a man had stolen her heart, given her a baby, then took off, never to be heard from again.

But her mom had lied to her.

I couldn't begin to imagine how Wren must have felt when learning the truth about her father, a man who'd given her mom money to have sex. Nothing more than a transaction wrapped up in a worthless condom.

She hadn't been a love child but a mistake.

"Shit." A tear leaked from my eye, and I swiped it away while huffing an exhale through my tight throat.

How the fuck did you respond to someone pouring out their soul like that? Bearing everything about themselves they saw as a dirty sin?

I had no ability to type out all the words filling my mind.

So I didn't.

Chapter 19

Wren

I'd told Jenny everything on the ride home and wished I'd done so while at work the week before. She never would have asked her cousin to hook us up with a couple of his escorts and caused one of the most emotional nights of my life.

Well, the beginning of it, anyway.

Jenny had explained what Blake told her and that Jarod had verified his words.

But still.

By that point, I'd been worked up, reminded again of being nothing more than a prostitute's oops, and I had trouble setting aside that I'd felt lied to even if I hadn't.

When I'd gotten home, Mom had been sleeping, or so Nancy and I thought.

She hadn't woken in the morning after my restless night lying in bed and staring at my old bedroom's stained ceiling. When the hospice nurse came at my call, she told me Mom had slipped into unconsciousness and that it would only be a matter of hours or days before she passed.

I'd spent all of Sunday morning and early afternoon

sitting beside her, regretting that we wouldn't have another conversation. That I couldn't beg forgiveness for my behavior after her confession. I couldn't ask her what she thought I should do about Blake.

Not that she would have had any good advice to offer.

Or maybe her past might have gifted her insight in the way I ought to go forward.

Either way, I would never know, and that brought on the beginnings of grief over the woman who had never gone out of her way to show me love or assure me of it with words.

And I finally understood why.

How did you love a child you'd never wanted, another person you had to supply with the barest essentials when you could barely do so for yourself? At least she hadn't aborted me and had done her best to keep me healthy—even while ignoring her own body and mind.

But if she hadn't wanted me, she could have easily ridden herself of the burden of raising me. Perhaps she had loved me and just didn't know how to show it?

Talk about emotional turmoil.

The roughest week lay ahead of me, and since I wanted the whole Blake situation off my plate, I decided to tell him the truth and offer an apology. That, at least, would ease my mind of one issue I faced.

Same as that morning I had unloaded in his ear all those weeks ago, I poured out by text what I'd learned, offering an apology for my behavior.

I hoped he would understand my reaction. I also found myself wanting his forgiveness.

Mom's chest barely moved, but I still sat and stared at it after setting my phone aside, waiting for the final rise and fall.

My cell rang, but she didn't flinch.

Blake.

Swallowing hard at the unwanted butterflies in my belly, I got up and left Mom's room before answering. "Hi."

"Hey, little birdie."

I rolled my eyes, but my lips twitched upward the slightest bit at the hint of relief and maybe even happiness in his voice. So he was no longer as devastated as he'd appeared the night before when I'd thought he'd been acting.

Blake really did like me.

Too bad I wasn't in a good space for anything more than friendship.

I settled onto the sagging couch. "You read my text?"

"Yeah. I wasn't sure how to respond other than apology accepted, and your reaction was totally understandable, so I decided to call. I hope that's okay?"

"Of course." Closing my eyes, I tipped my head back, liking how the rumble of his voice in my ear offered a sense of...what felt like security. Like I knew where I stood with Blake, that I could trust him with my emotions.

"How's your mom?"

My chest tightened over the fact he wanted to hear about her first. "Unconscious." I shrugged even though he couldn't see me. "The hospice nurse said it could be hours or days. Some stubborn souls hang on way longer than they should be able to without water."

"Do you need anything? How can I help?"

Stinging attacked my eyes. "I'm good, and it's just a waiting game now."

"Well if there's anything I can do, please let me know."

"I will," I whispered through the tightness in my throat.

"So, your text said Jenny explained my connection with Elite Escorts, but I'd like to tell you the whole of it—if you're interested in even hearing."

Anything to pass the time, I wanted to mutter but didn't since there was something more inside me that wanted to just sit and talk to the man who had been thoughtful in all his notes and small gifts.

"I'd like to hear the truth from you," I said instead.

"Micah Fox, the owner of EE, has been a friend of mine for years, but it wasn't until the Friday after I met you that he talked me into helping him out of a jam."

I listened without interruption as Blake explained about the couple who enjoyed being watched, but he kept the details to himself. I expected sitting in on a live porn show of two people desperately in love—his words—would be a turn-on for a guy. I was sure he enjoyed it, otherwise why would he have agreed to continue going to their home whenever they requested one of the Elites for a night of voyeurism?

I couldn't fault the man for his choice. While a straight couple wouldn't do a whole lot for me, if two gay guys asked me to sit in the shadows and watch them make love...yes, please. No doubt I would squirm in the best way possible and get myself off once I returned home.

Blake had also been eye candy for some rich foreigners along with Reid who also wasn't an Elite, and Jarod, the guy he'd been with the night before. As for Jenny's request, Micah's men had been booked, but Jarod's client for the night had cancelled, leaving him the sole man available to hang with two women at Encore.

"I agreed to tag along since there was no expectation of sex. That's something I never would have done, Wren."

"I'm sure you don't need any assistance in getting laid," I said.

"So you *do* think I'm hot."

I could hear the grin in his teasing voice and plucked at a loose thread on the cushion beside me. "You know you are."

Time for his fourth attempt…

"I'm all done with Elite," he said instead of asking me out like I'd expected. "I told Micah last night."

"Okay." I waited, sure he was building up to it.

"So how are you handling work and classes this week?"

I blinked. "Huh?"

"Do you have vacation or sick time and are you able to access that summer course online?"

"I had my final on Friday," I said, sure he would try to sneak an invite to dinner or something in before the end of our conversation. Why else would he have called? "That's what Jenny and I were celebrating."

"That's got to be a load off your mind. How do you think you did?"

"Well enough. I studied the best I could all things considered, and the test wasn't as hard as I'd expected."

"When does the fall quarter start?"

I settled into talking the minutes away, filling Blake in on my life in ways I began to believe he might actually be interested in. His questions sounded genuine, as though he really wanted to get to know me, not just get his hands on me again.

We discussed my job at the pharmacy where I worked with Jenny and how I'd changed my hours with the promise of full-time again once matters with my mom were settled.

I checked in on her after twenty or so minutes on the phone, and her chest still moved with shallow breaths.

Back in the living room, I took advantage of Blake helping me pass the next hour away by asking him questions —about Harper's Construction and his life outside work.

I expected bragging, his usual arrogance, but he simply spoke facts about his daily living without any suggestive tones or teasing. And there were zero sexual innuendos or hints of flirting.

Surprised by the side of Blake I hadn't heard about before, I found myself enjoying our conversation.

We even got into the nerdy part of his inner workings, and though I wasn't a sci-fi fan like him, we found common ground in the entertainment aspect of finding escape from reality.

I'd never heard of Dianna Troi, an actress he told me I reminded him of, and he'd never heard of Annie Kelly, my favorite author.

We liked the same food—Thai and pineapple on pizza. We were also both night owls, needing at least two cups of coffee in the morning in order to function. He loved the Sox, and I adored the Bruins even though I didn't know much about hockey. I just had a thing for big burly men who could move on ice as easily as they could on dry ground. That took serious talent.

Two hours passed before I realized the time and that my stomach growled.

"Thank you for calling rather than texting me back," I told him from where I'd curled up on my side on the couch.

"Was I a good distraction?" he asked.

"You were so much more than that," I said. "Please don't think I only stayed on the phone to help pass the time."

"I meant what I said about if you need anything, Wren."

A flutter rippled through my belly at the low tone of his voice saying my name. "Thank you."

"Keep in touch, okay?"

That was it then, a simple goodbye.

Silence once more settled in my ear as I set my cell aside. He hadn't asked me out. Was it because of my situation or because knowing the truth of who I was, he recognized I wasn't good enough for someone like him?

I was actually...disappointed he hadn't shown any interest when he'd been so set on it before, but I pushed that sentiment aside.

I had enough to worry about.

Hand beneath my cheek, I scanned over the small living room I'd played in as a child. With all of Mom's junk I'd yet to rifle through, I couldn't see much of the rug I used to sit on with the one doll and cracked tea set Mom had found me alongside the road.

What a cleanup job I had ahead of me...

Exhaling heavily, I pushed up off the couch and checked in on Mom again.

Seeing she still breathed, I returned to the living room and started to bag up items I could drop off in a donation bin up at the shopping plaza a few blocks away.

I couldn't keep my mind from replaying the conversation with Blake and admitting he was a good guy at heart. I'd definitely misjudged him. Just because he hadn't dated anyone for an extended period of time and enjoyed having women fall all over him didn't make him a bad person.

What single man wouldn't live it up if such a future hovered before them?

A bright guy, considering his name and station in society.

Mentally locking my emotions up tight toward him, I

decided I would accept him into my life as a friend and keep all other feels suppressed.

White trash had no place alongside upper class like him and his family.

I knew where I'd come from, and though I would eventually rise above my station financially, I would never belong in his world.

Chapter 20

Blake

Even though I felt emotionally drained, my two-hour conversation with Wren zinged energy through my limbs. I hated what she faced but couldn't squash my own happiness.

Talking to her had accomplished more than I'd expected. I'd hoped to just offer comfort and maybe even find a way to help her get through the week but had gained so much more.

Learning what she liked.

Hearing how she laughed, because yeah, I'd gotten her to think outside of grief and work for a little while.

Experiencing a connection even if only through friendship.

For now.

I toyed with the words, knowing we had enough in common, that we had an ease in communicating, that would lend toward more if given the chance.

Once things settled for her, I would maybe try again, but she needed a friend, not some guy attempting to get his hands on her body for a second time.

Sure, I wanted that, fucking lusted for it, but there was that sense of desire for more, a yearning to connect beyond the physical that lead my thoughts forward with Wren.

Heart and mind set on growing that aspect between us, I kept in touch.

Monday over my lunch break, I texted to check in on her mom.

Her body stubbornly clung to life.

I sent a few words of encouragement, reminding her again to reach out to me if she needed someone.

Tuesday went almost the same, but she called me that night. Our conversation wasn't as long as Sunday's, and I could hear the exhaustion in her voice.

"I'm sure she won't make it through the week," Wren said, her voice soft and almost hollow-sounding, "and I can't decide if I'm happy or sad about it. I mean, I don't want her suffering to drag on, but..."

"But?" I pushed when the silence reached on too long.

Wren exhaled loudly, and I wished I could pull her into a hug rather than sit like a lump on my couch alone in the dark.

"Sunday is my birthday," Wren almost whispered, "and even though she hadn't wanted a kid, she always found a way to make the day special. Most of the time, it was a stale cake on sale at the grocery store. One year she got two balloons and strawberry cupcake mix from the local food pantry. There wasn't any frosting, but they were the best thing I've ever tasted."

The tears in her voice clogged up my throat, not that I'd have offered her wishes for a happy birthday all things considered. I wanted to take her out for dinner but didn't ask. The third time hadn't been the charm, so why would the fourth?

Even though we'd made progress in...whatever it was we were becoming, she'd made it clear she wasn't interested in me that way. My wishes for more needed to take a back seat, and I would take whatever I could get.

Wednesday, Wren didn't reply to my text in the morning or again the one I sent around dinner time.

Thursday repeated the same lack of communication, and I began to worry.

I expected her mom had passed, and I longed to be there for Wren. Offer assistance in whatever she had to take care of.

But she had Jenny and the neighbor, I reminded myself. People who had been in her life longer than I had. Real friends, not just some random acquaintance who'd been after her ass pre-friend zone.

I had no wish to bug her, but I couldn't handle not knowing how she was doing. My call went straight to voice-mail, and I stumbled through my thoughts, reminding her I was there if she needed a friend.

The word felt sour on my tongue since I definitely felt more for her.

Friday morning, I left one of my encouragement notes on her bottom step and kept an eye out while working.

She never stopped by her apartment—same as every morning that week.

Wren had told me where her mom lived, but considering the lines she'd drawn in the sand about who I was to her, I didn't go looking for her at the apartment complex down in Lynn.

If Wren wanted or needed me, she would text or call.

Having to leave it at that, I went out with the guys on Friday night.

Colton actually dragged his in-love ass away from his

silver fox and curvy goddess but couldn't stop grinning. He and Reid shared a high-top table with me at our favorite bar, and I couldn't help but envy my friends.

Reid enjoyed the fuck out of the single life, always perusing the ladies like I used to do, and Colton had found the love he'd been looking for.

Colton acted like an antsy kid on the hard stool across from me, shifting so damn much Reid finally mentioned it.

"Either your daddy spanked your ass last night or he railed it," Reid said, his dark eyes twinkling like they always did when he teased.

Colton laughed when he would have given Reid shit about the whole daddy teasing a few weeks earlier. "Both."

"TMI," I muttered and sucked down a few swigs of my beer. I had no issue with who a person loved or enjoyed in bed because it didn't matter to me, but I wasn't interested in hearing the details.

"How are things going with Hudson and Madeline?" Reid asked while I checked my cell for the hundredth or so time that day.

Still no word from Wren.

"Fucking phenomenal," Colton replied, still grinning.

I'd never seen him so damn happy and wasn't about to complain since he'd been a grumpy bear all summer long, pining for the couple he'd fallen for.

He'd found love, and something greenish rose up inside me every time I caught him smiling on the job.

Envy.

But I wasn't jealous over Reid getting women whenever he went out looking.

I had no interest in women outside Wren. At all.

Fuck.

Rubbing a hand along my scruff, I considered how long

it had been since I'd gotten laid. Well before I'd had Wren's tiny hips in my hands while losing my mind over how her ass suckled on my dick.

"Goddamn," I whisper-groaned, having to adjust my junk beneath the table.

"You alright over there?" Colton asked, and I shook my head.

"Bastard needs to get some," Reid told our friend.

I did, but not in the way he suggested.

Colton studied me across the table. "You okay?"

"I'm hung up on Wren—same as you were on Hudson and his wife before they invited you into their bed and stole your heart."

One of his eyebrows arched upward. "Seriously?"

"Yeah." I sat back, holding the beer bottle with both hands atop the table. "It's definitely more than just wanting to get my hands on her body too."

"She *is* one sweet morsel."

I shot a glare over at Reid who smirked at me. "Don't get any ideas, Sully."

He barked a laugh. "I wouldn't ever do that to you."

I knew that but felt more possessive over Wren than I had any other woman we'd shared over the years.

"I can't wait for the day you fall for some woman so I can give you shit," I told Reid.

Colton chuckled. "Same."

Reid had given him a ton of it while he'd been the one moping on Friday nights.

"So what's up with you and Wren?" Colton asked.

I filled him in on what had gone down the weekend before and everything leading up to my current situation of hating the silence from her.

"You should swing by," he suggested.

"I don't know if she sees me as a good enough friend to just drop in like that. Especially with her mom's situation. My luck, I'd go to knock as the coroner is wheeling her mom's body out or something."

He grimaced. "Yeah, that would be awkward as fuck."

"I'm assuming she passed earlier this week though, and Wren is too busy with details or too upset to chat with someone who's not..." I trailed off, not sure how to label what we were or weren't. "This fucking sucks." I tipped back my beer and finished it up.

"Did you text her today?" Reid asked, and I nodded.

"This morning."

Our waitress showed up with a tray of the food we'd ordered, so I focused on filling my empty stomach and making it through the hours ahead until I could sleep and forget about the sweet woman who haunted my mind.

Chapter 21

Wren

The death rattle had started Tuesday during the evening, and not long after the sun rose Wednesday morning, Mom's chest stopped moving. I'd made the call to hospice, then sat in numb silence, waiting for them to come and take her body way.

Even though a ton of details awaited me, my mind had quieted, exhausted and numb from being awake half the night.

I'd stood aside and let the nurse do what she had to, the first pricks of grief stinging my eyes when two guys had showed up to transfer Mom's body to a gurney and wheel her from the apartment.

Rather than going outside with them, I'd stayed put.

It seemed like hours had slid by as I'd riffled through paperwork I'd already straightened, but I'd been beyond the point of tired and couldn't sleep. Finally, my body had given in, and it wasn't until the following day after sleeping hard for twelve hours straight that I'd begun the process of putting things in order.

I hadn't texted anyone. Hadn't replied to Jenny or Blake, the only two people to reach out to me in my silence.

Perhaps some part of me had thought denying Mom being gone would make going forward easier.

I'd grieved more than I expected.

Mom might not have met my emotional needs as a child or young adult, but I realized she *had* loved me in the only way she probably knew how, considering her own upbringing. I regretted not talking to her about my feelings, and the sense of unfinished business between us that would never be put to rest laid heavy on my heart.

I'd become an orphan without a single family member to call my own.

I had no one but myself.

The reality of loneliness hovered over my mind like a dark shroud, and I wallowed in self-pity.

Focusing on one step at a time, I made it through the following days, getting shit done until all that was left was emptying out Mom's apartment. I donated what I could, but dozens of bags and trash along with the furniture that was in too poor of shape to sell or even offer to anyone in need still remained.

Jenny called after two days of ignored texts, and I filled her in on what was going on. She offered to help clean Mom's place since she had off on Sunday.

I ordered a dumpster for delivery, and Saturday night, I sat at the small table in Mom's kitchen, so damn exhausted I couldn't drive back to my own place to sleep.

One more night. One more day.

Then I could finally focus on the upcoming final year of school and getting back to work at the pharmacy.

Tomorrow is my birthday.

I swallowed hard at the reminder that flitted through my mind without prompting.

Neither Nancy nor Jenny knew, and I wasn't about to tell them when they showed up at ten the next morning to help me clean out the apartment. How we would handle the furniture, I wasn't sure, but maybe I could grab a couple of the teenagers who hung around out on the front stoop of the apartment building. Twenty bucks a piece would probably get them to assist us for the half hour or so it would take to get the bigger pieces into the trash.

I had both the dumpster and the apartment keys until Monday night when I'd promised the building owner I would hand them over. But I planned to buckle down and get shit done until I fell from exhaustion—and I told my boss I'd be back to work Tuesday.

Blake had offered to help me in any way I needed, but I didn't expect he'd be interested in lugging bags of trash down three flights of stairs. I realized I needed to at least call him and tell him about my mom, but I feared breaking into tears.

The memory of his kindness and those notes he'd left me made me wish for things I couldn't have, and my emotions were already on the edge. If I heard his voice, the sensitivity I knew would show toward me, I would end up crying again.

No man wanted to listen to a woman cry.

So I didn't call. Instead, I finally sent him a text to let him know my mom had passed.

Of course, texting back would never be enough for him. Instead, he rang immediately.

Slowly inhaling to steady myself, I let my cell ring three times before answering. "Hi."

"I'm so sorry, Wren."

Fuck, his voice had to rasp in the way that revealed my own sadness affected him.

My eyes hazed over. "Thanks."

"How are you holding up?"

"M'kay, I guess," I managed, my throat tight and chin trembling.

"Is there anything I can do for you?" He sounded so sincere, so worried for me...

Twin tears slid down my cheeks, and I choked on a sob.

"Shit, Wren. I'm sorry. I didn't mean to make you cry."

"I-I'm okay." I swiped wetness from my cheeks, breathing deeply to get ahold of myself. "Th-There's a lot to do," I managed through stilted inhales and swallows against more tears. "Cleaning out her apartment t-tomorrow. I rented a dumpster. There's j-just so much." It took me awhile to get the words past my lips without outright sobbing.

He murmured a few things I couldn't really hear while I wiped my face on my sleeve.

Blowing out a lungful of annoyance over being so damn emotional, I told myself to get it together.

"I have off at the pharmacy until Tuesday," I said, "so it shouldn't be a problem. After that, I can focus on the upcoming semester and work."

"Have you been by your apartment lately? I haven't seen you stop in during the day."

"No." I closed my eyes and lay my cheek on the table, slumped once more with exhaustion.

"Want me to swing by and water your plants?"

My damn throat went tight again. "You would do that for me?"

"Of course, Wren. That's what friends are for."

More tears escaped my eyes.

Blake Harper considered me a friend, and I loved that he did.

A smile wobbled on my lips as I told him where I hid my spare key, and a few minutes later, I once more sat in silence.

But I didn't feel as alone. The memory of Blake's warm voice, his words of encouragement before hanging up assuring me that I would get the job done before Monday night. He reminded me that I had fire and stubbornness enough to complete my task.

I hadn't given him shit for calling me stubborn.

Instead, I appreciated he saw that part of me as an asset and not a negative like my ex had.

Somewhat invigorated, I crawled onto my old single mattress on the floor and closed my eyes regardless of the fact the sun hadn't fully set.

Dreams of Blake wavered like sunbeams through the clouds of my dreams, and when I woke up in the pre-dawn light, I lay still, searching my emotions, my feelings about the day ahead.

Within a matter of hours, all of Mom's possessions would be gone, same as her voice and her presence.

But I would choose to remember her with fondness. Maybe the good thoughts would be enough to keep me company as I faced the rest of my life without anyone on earth I could call my family.

Chapter 22

Blake

Wren had told me about her mom's place, how she'd been a hoarder for years. I expected the task of cleaning the apartment out wouldn't be easy. And with how tiny Wren was, it would be one hell of a job to tackle.

She sounded exhausted too.

I hadn't asked if I could help, because knowing Wren, she would turn me down like she did for everything else.

But she couldn't stop me from showing up with a crew in tow, and I doubted she would embarrass me by sending us away.

Hell, even if she attempted to, I anticipated putting the stubborn woman in her place.

After getting off the phone with her, I headed north in my truck to see to her plants, and the sweet scent of berries wafted over me when I stepped into her dark, quiet apartment. She trusted me to go into her personal space unchaperoned, so I chose right and kept from snooping, no matter how desperately I wanted to look into every corner and crevice of her life to learn more about her.

The plants in the kitchen window drooped, and I whispered a few words of encouragement while watering them, hoping they would survive. The last thing she needed was something else dying on her.

Once finished, I grasped the door handle to exit but paused, eyeing the place through the sunset creeping in the window above her small table. The couch sat empty, and I allowed myself a moment to relive what had started there.

My hands on her skin, my mouth on her neck.

Life twitched in my groin, and I allowed myself a few moments to reflect and enjoy the memory of the one time she had allowed me access to her body.

My feet shifted before I made a move in my head, and I found myself in her bedroom doorway.

Her queen-sized bed appeared neatly made, sheets tucked and two pillows fluffed.

I stepped closer and stood in the spot I had that night, seeing in my mind's eye how she'd melted over Reid's chest and gifted me her ass.

My dick turned to fuck mode within seconds, but I ignored the ache simmering in my balls. Instead, I kept my hands at my sides while reliving the experience of sinking into her. Hearing her cries. Watching her shudder and shiver beneath me.

She'd been exquisite. Stunning in taking her release from me. Us.

My entire body throbbed to give her more, to offer comfort in a million different ways.

But even if she never allowed me that opportunity again, I still wanted to be her friend. Help her. Offer my ear, my muscles, or whatever she needed to help see her through life.

I wasn't just in lust with the woman.

I was falling for her.

That truth trailed after me as I headed south in my truck, quickly shooting off a text to see if Colton was at the Youngs' house and not fucking around.

He replied, telling me to swing by.

I detoured off Route 1 a few minutes later and put through a call on speaker phone to Reid.

Surprised he answered since he was an Elite for Micah again that night, I told him what I planned for the morning.

He agreed to help without question like I knew he would.

I then called my mother's old housekeeper, ending our conversation when I pulled up in front of the Youngs'.

Things set in place to have Wren's mom's apartment scrubbed by professionals on Sunday afternoon, I hopped from my truck and strode up to the Youngs' front door.

Colton answered. "Come on in." He clasped my shoulder in greeting as I passed him into the tiled entryway.

Hudson and Madeline sat on the couch in the living room to the right. The TV was on but muted as they both glanced over at me. Hudson dipped his head in greeting while his wife smiled.

I'd heard through Colton that they felt they owed me the world for assigning the deck job they'd hired us for to Colton. Because of his laboring in the hot sun for two weeks earlier that summer, they'd found the third they hadn't been aware they wanted.

They both stood as Colton led me into the living room.

Hudson shook my hand, but Madeline threw her arms around me, squeezing me tight. "Thank you," she said, her eyes shining with sudden tears.

"I really had nothing to do with this." I motioned between the three of them.

"Bullshit," Colton said, elbowing me.

"Colton said you wanted to talk to us?" Hudson prompted, his voice gruff but not unkind as he once more took a seat.

Madeline curled up against his side—and Colton did the same on the other.

I grinned while sitting on the recliner, taking in their contented faces, envious of how their hands rested on each other.

Fuck, did I want that in my life. Complete comfort, knowing someone loved me for me. Accepted all the parts of me that had nothing to do with money and status.

If only.

Wren and I definitely had that potential. She hadn't laughed or made one comment about me loving Star Trek or that I thought she looked like Diana, my first Hollywood crush.

I pushed the sweet thoughts aside and told them about Wren. What she'd gone through since her mom had become ill, how she'd been caring for her the previous couple of weeks while holding down a job and finishing up her summer course.

"You're in love with her," Madeline stated without a hint of question in her voice.

I opened my mouth to refute her claim but closed it without uttering a word.

I'd never been in love with a woman before, but was it possible that desire I felt for Wren was that four-letter word my mom and dad always asked me about finding?

"Well, she deserves to be happy in every way," I finally said, shifting forward to lean my forearms on my knees. I clasped my hands, studying the fingers that had touched her skin. "And I want to wrap her up in my arms and protect her. Cherish her. Make her laugh. Hold her when she cries. I could sit and listen to her for hours, watch her expressive face, and grasp hold of the butterflies she brings to life in my stomach."

"Like I said," Madeline said, pulling my focus upward. She smiled kindly. "Love."

I swallowed hard, glancing over at Colton.

He smirked. "Looks like Boston's most sought after bachelor playboy is no longer on the market."

"She won't go out with me, and at this point, I'm done trying to talk her into it. I'd rather be her friend than nothing at all."

Madeline made a sweet, quiet, sigh-like sound, and Hudson tucked her in tighter, kissing her temple.

"Tell us what you need," Hudson said, so I laid out my plans.

All three were on board with helping out, but it was the final piece I wasn't sure we could pull off due to the late hour.

Once I shared what I had in mind, Madeline's face lit. "Oh, what a *perfect* idea!"

She hopped up and grabbed Colton's hand, dragging him off the couch. "Be a good boy and help me."

Colton shot me a wink, grabbed her ass, and scurried along like a dog hot on his bitch's heels.

They disappeared into the kitchen, leaving me alone with Hudson.

He chuckled, shaking his head.

If loving Wren was what I felt, I couldn't imagine it doubled.

"How do you do it?" I asked.

"Do what?" He turned his gaze on me, his hazel eyes a lot less closed off.

"Love two people? Not get jealous? Fulfill their needs in equal measures?"

He laid both arms across the back of the couch as though fully confident. "It's not easy, but as long as there's honesty and open communication, we do just fine."

"Only fine?" I couldn't help but toss out, one of my eyebrows arching.

A gruff chuckle twitched his salt and pepper beard. "Some days, those two are double the trouble, but they're also twice the pleasure."

And that was where I ended the conversation, because I had no wish to hear about my buddy's sex life with a married couple he'd weaseled his way between and seemed to fit with like a glove.

"So, tomorrow?" I asked, standing up to head into the kitchen to see if I could help complete the final step of my plan.

"We'll be there," Hudson promised.

Chapter 23

Wren

The dumpster got dropped off at seven sharp, and I started to retrieve bags within minutes of the guy leaving. At least the elevator was in working order, keeping me from having to traipse up and down three flights of stairs.

That would have killed me.

But with countless bags, boxes, and old bins to lug outside, I expected it would easily take until sundown before I finished. Nancy wouldn't be a whole lot of help with her old, achy knees, but I wasn't about to turn away her offer.

On my fourth trip outside into the cool morning air, I stopped short just outside the complex's door as a big silver truck I recognized entered the parking lot.

Blake.

Heat flushed through me, definitely settling in my cheeks, but it was the relief, the thankfulness rushing through my body that made my legs weak. Two other trucks followed along behind, parking beside him.

I tossed the bags into the trash, my pulse fluttering and

my throat tight.

Blake and Reid hopped from his truck, two others I recognized from the job site across from my apartment climbed from the second, and the third held another of Blake's employees, a blonde woman and an older guy.

All seven approached me, and I rubbed my damp palms down the ratty jeans I'd worn. Blake led them, his eyes the slightest bit wary as though unsure if I would be mad for his showing up without asking first.

"I brought some help," he said, coming to stand directly in front of me. "Is that okay?"

I managed to nod but didn't trust my voice.

His face split into a grin, and he turned to introduce me to everyone.

Hudson and Madeline held hands—and she slipped her free one into Colton's, tugging him against her side.

My mind immediately went to my favorite Annie Kelly book, and I almost swooned. Could they be any cuter?

Smiling through my teary eyes, I met Brian and Eddie, and the second Blake finished with the name exchanging, Reid stepped in and wrapped me up in a hug, lifting me clear off the ground.

"I'm sorry for your loss, Wren," he whispered against my ear.

I melted into his hard chest, filling my lungs with the scent of soap, and a twinge of arousal slid through me at the memory of the night we'd shared with Blake. Or maybe it was the thought of Blake being inside my body that brought life to my core.

Either way, I soaked in the moment a little selfishly, clinging tighter to his muscular back than I should have. The last thing I needed was Reid believing I wanted him.

Blake cleared his throat, and Reid chuckled, quickly setting me back down.

Lips in a thin line, Blake glared at him.

Another lick of heat slid through me, dampening my palms again. I shut down ideas of Blake going all possessive of my ass. "I really appreciate you all coming down here to help me out. It...means a lot." My lips once more wobbled as I met Blake's navy blues. So much warmth radiated from his gaze that my fingers itched to reach out and touch him.

He kept his hands to himself, so I did too.

"Put us to work, Wren," he said before I could think too much on my disappointment in the lack of physical touch, the offer of comfort like Reid had willingly given.

"Well." I tried for a more stable smile. "I'll lead the way —and I apologize in advance for the mess."

Embarrassment crept up my cheeks as all eight of us crammed into the elevator. The stench of stale cigarettes and mildew wrinkled my nose, but I'd become accustomed to it. I couldn't begin to imagine what Blake and his friends thought.

Pushing aside my concerns, I focused on the fact I had help—big time. All thanks to the mass of muscle standing beside me, pressed up against my shoulder and hip because of the tight quarters.

Arousal slid over my skin, and I allowed myself to enjoy the moment. Besides, no room existed for me to shift away.

The second the doors slid open, I breathed easier, bolting forward to escape his delicious, spicy scent and gentle touch.

"So this is it," I said, leading the way into Mom's dingy apartment. I didn't turn to look at anyone since I feared their reactions to the amount of trash in the tiny two-bedroom. "Everything that's bagged and in boxes goes into the dumpster. All the furniture needs to go too."

The men set to work, Blake taking charge and bossing everyone around.

Madeline clasped my elbow as I went to grab another bag, and she studied my face. "How are you doing?"

Her tone, the empathy in her blue eyes hit me like a train, and tears immediately started to roll down my cheeks.

She wrapped an arm around my shoulders and led me into the closest bedroom—mine—and quietly shut the door behind us.

"Go ahead and let it out, Wren," she murmured, offering me a hug.

The sweet scent of honeysuckle filled my lungs with every gasped inhale, and I clung to her as though we'd been friends forever. I'd only been held by a woman a handful of times in my life, and the softness of her breasts felt so... motherly in the way I'd always imagined a mom ought to be.

I broke down and didn't bother trying to stop the grief I'd attempted to squash until I rested against her, spent.

She rubbed my back. "Better?"

Sighing, I nodded and stepped away.

Madeline clutched my shoulders. "Now. Let's clean up your face and smeared glasses, then we'll pretend to help all that sexy muscle out there."

I actually snickered at her wink while pulling off my glasses to wipe them on my shirt. "Can I ask you a question?"

"Of course. Anything."

"Are you with Hudson *and* Colton?"

Her crooked smirk lit her eyes. "Yes. Hudson and I got married years ago, and Colton is our boyfriend."

"As in both of yours, the whole crossing of swords thing?"

"He's Hudson's good boy." Another wink came from Madeline, and I bit back a snicker.

"Have you ever read any of Annie Kelly's books?" I asked, putting my glasses back on my face.

"I've never heard of her."

Linking my arm through Madeline's, I started toward my bedroom door. "She's going to be your new favorite author. Trust me."

The guys had already cleared out most of the living room, and even though my heart swelled with gratitude, I managed to keep my tears in check.

Blake caught my gaze as he stepped back into the apartment, and I mouthed another *Thank you.*

His smile sent tingles clear through to my toes like an extra dose of cleansing rain after my moment of grief.

"Colton, help me with the couch." Blake grabbed one end, Colton picked up the other, and they disappeared through the door.

Madeline and I both sighed at the same time—then burst into laughter.

Surreal.

That was what it felt like having Blake Harper show up with an army to make my life easier.

But had he done it hoping to get me to see him in a different light, as more than the friends I felt we'd become? Or was he genuine about wanting to nourish the budding connection we'd found?

He looked at me like he desired more. Every single time our paths crossed in the following two hours, those navy blues expressed longing that rushed a similar sentiment through me.

At ten, he told us all to take a break.

We all sat outside in the fresh air rather than in Mom's apartment. Madeline and Blake went over to the Youngs' truck to grab the case of water he said they'd brought while Colton asked me about the upcoming semester of school.

Hudson, Reid, and the other two guys settled on the curb, legs stretched out and relaxed.

I kept my back to Blake since I wouldn't be able to stop staring at him. The last thing I needed was for him to get any ideas.

While part of me had definitely softened toward Blake and I realized he might not be like I'd originally assumed, trust didn't come easily. Holding him off at arm's length would be best.

Besides, I had school to think about, and there was no room in my life for distraction—

"Happy birthday to you!" Blake's singing jerked me around, and everyone else joined in the song.

He held a tray of cupcakes with pink frosting, and the warmth in his eyes as he drew near lanced the sweetest ache through my chest. A single candle flickered, and I tore my stare off Blake's face to focus on keeping from crying again.

I swore all I could do was leak tears and fight off exhaustion.

A break would be nice...

So that was what I wished for while blowing out the candle.

Reid slung an arm around my shoulder and smacked a smooch against my cheek. "Happy birthday, sweet girl."

The guys all grabbed cupcakes off Blake's tray while Madeline handed out bottles of water.

Once everyone settled with their snacks made by the owner of Mads's Sweet Treats, Blake set the tray aside but held two cupcakes in his hands. He offered one to me, which I took, the caress of his fingers along mine sending a shiver up my arm.

I couldn't help the threat of tears. "Thank you, Blake, for everything. I can't..." Swallowing hard, I tried to smile. The sight of his gorgeous face wavered as wetness flooded my eyes.

He swiped his thumb over my cheek, catching the first tear. "I couldn't have you thinking that no one remembered. I wanted to make this day as special as possible."

He had accomplished what he'd set out to do and then some.

I stepped in close and wrapped one arm around his waist, pressing my cheek against his chest. Eyes closed, I listened to his heartbeat. Filled my lungs with the scent of soap and sweat.

Whatever red flags I'd thought I'd seen waving in my head dissolved.

Blake Harper was a *damn* good man.

Chapter 24

Blake

I hadn't meant to make Wren cry. Seeing big tears roll from beneath her glasses to trickle down her cheek fucking hurt my heart.

Madeline had it right. I was damn gone on Wren. There wasn't anything I wouldn't do for her.

And feeling her wrapped around me, hugging me tight with one arm?

Heaven.

I rested my chin atop her head and wished I wasn't holding the cupcake so I could squeeze her into me with both of mine arms. But I took advantage of the moment, etching into my memory the feel of her smallness pressed against my front. How slender she was with just enough softness my body recognized *woman* in every way possible.

Once more, she fit so damn perfectly against me while I cradled her upper back. She damn well belonged there too.

Had things been different between us and we were anywhere but in front of six of my friends, I'd have hefted her up off the ground so she could settle her legs around my waist.

I would span her ass cheeks with my hands, map out the feel of their roundness. I would nose along her neck and breathe in the scent of sweet berries. And I would definitely finally claim those lips I'd been dreaming about kissing since the first day we'd met.

My dick woke the fuck up, and I couldn't help it. There was no point in trying to hide what she did to me—it was too damn obvious—but I didn't shift to make it more apparent or try to grind for a more friction either.

I simply stood still, owning my body's response without apology.

Wren lingered regardless of my thickening dick against her belly as though accepting the truth of my desire and not being disgusted by it.

Hope swelled, making me harder, and I swallowed a groan, fighting off the need to press even closer.

The seconds didn't drag on nearly long enough even though every heartbeat throbbed for just a few more moments with her against me. I could have kept her right there all day.

Too soon, Wren stepped back, her cheeks pink but no longer wet. She wouldn't meet my eyes but focused on the cupcake in her shaking hand.

"Madeline and Colton made them last night," I said to fill the silence—the rasp in my voice matching the unsteadiness in my body. "They're strawberry, your favorite."

Her face lifted, the look on her face slamming me in the chest.

Happiness. Appreciation. And maybe even a little acceptance that made my feet itch to dance, something I never did.

"You caught that," she murmured, a soft, genuine smile curving her lips.

I nodded, my breath gone from being the focal point of her existence in that moment.

A soft huff of laughter escaped her as though surprised.

I hadn't forgotten anything she'd told me, I'd committed her words to memory. Every little tidbit about Wren held importance. Her expressions, each emotion. I wanted to see them all. Feel them. Experience them with her.

When she bit into the cupcake, I had to look away, so damn overcome with love I didn't know what the fuck to do with myself.

Reid smirked at me.

Madeline winked.

I downed my cupcake in two bites, grabbed one of the waters from the package nearby, and uncapped and then sucked it down, tearing my mind off Wren. Tough to do when she stood so damn close, but I managed.

We finished emptying her mom's place within the next two hours. Jenny and Nancy had shown up to help although the older woman didn't do much beyond boss the boys around and flirt nonstop.

Not quite noon and we all stood outside, saying our goodbyes.

Wren went to one person at a time, hugging and offering her thanks. Madeline suggested they get together for lunch one day, and Wren's eyes filled with wetness for about the hundredth time that morning as she agreed.

Reid and I were the last in line, and I tried not to get possessive and shit when his hug lingered as the others trailed off to their cars.

He knew about my final plan for the day, so he ambled toward the truck after telling her goodbye, leaving me and Wren alone.

Before shit could get awkward, I pulled an envelope from my back pocket and handed it to her.

"What's this?" she asked, flipping it over to find my scrawled writing of her name on the front.

"Birthday present."

Pink stained her cheeks. "You didn't have to get me anything."

"Yes I did." Shoving my hands into my jeans' pockets, I watched her slender fingers work the tucked-in flap open.

Two gift certificates lay inside.

"A cleaning service?" she murmured, glancing up at me, a slight furrow between her eyebrows.

"They'll be here in a couple of hours to scrub the place from top to bottom, which means you're done for today," I stated firmly, not allowing for argument. "And that second one is for the spa at the Ritz Carlton downtown. I booked you a suite for tonight, so you won't have to do anything but crash and relax after a full afternoon of being pampered to death. They'll deliver dinner to your room, a bottle of wine...whatever you want. Then another appointment tomorrow morning to start your day off right."

"This is too much, Blake." She swallowed again, once more dropping her focus from my face, and I feared more tears even though I'd gotten used to seeing them in her eyes.

"You deserve to have your every need met without any effort on your part," I said quietly, leaning down the slightest bit into her personal space. "It's time to relax, and this is the best place in Boston to do that."

She lifted her head suddenly, cocking her head to the side, a hint of fire in her eyes I wasn't expecting. "And I suppose you're going to make a fourth attempt and ask if you can join me later?"

"Nope." I didn't even hesitate, didn't bother with my usual cocky flirting she had probably expected. "This isn't about me, Wren. It's simply my gift to a beautiful woman who needs space to rest."

Wren stared at me.

"I'm dead serious," I told her, straightening to my full height. "I'm not trying to buy my way into your heart or pants. There's no ulterior motive here, just a man wanting to make sure his friend thoroughly enjoys her birthday. Oh, and there's a limo on the way to pick you up," I tacked on.

She blinked. "What?"

"Limo. So you don't have to drive into Boston or home in the morning."

"But my car—"

"I'm taking it home for you. Reid will follow me in my truck."

"I-I don't know what to say, Blake."

I grinned, loving that she'd caved to what I wanted to give her. "You don't have to say anything. Just enjoy yourself. Let them soothe the stress and anxiety away so you're well rested for the upcoming week of work."

I wished I could be the one to pamper her but knew she wasn't yet ready to let me in. Maybe someday. There was no harm in hoping—but I wouldn't push.

Wren shuddered an exhale that sagged her shoulders, and she toyed with the envelope in her hands as though restless.

Did she want to hug me like she'd done with everyone else?

I stayed put. Hands still shoved in my pockets.

"Thanks again, Blake. Seriously. I appreciate all you've done for me. I owe you—"

"No you don't," I cut her off. "I did this because I care, not because I want anything in return."

She eyed me as though unsure of whether she ought to trust that statement or not, but I'd said what I could. It was up to her to trust me or not. Time would reveal my intentions though, since I had zero plans on asking her out.

If things were going to progress beyond friendship, it would be because she wanted it just as much as me.

The ball rested in her court.

She could pick it up and make me the happiest man alive or ignore it and keep me in the friend zone. I would learn to live with unrequited love if that ended up being the case.

The limo pulled into the complex's parking lot, giving me reason to turn away before she had to make a decision about hugging me or not.

Probably better that she hadn't. My dick couldn't take any more teasing.

Wren retrieved a few things from her car she'd packed up to head home and handed the keys over to me. "She's a piece of shit compared to what you're probably used to, but she'll make it home just fine."

"I'll take good care of her," I told her, already planning to hit a car wash and fill up the gas tank on the way to her place.

The limo driver held open the door, and I stood close as he shut her in.

Wren lowered the window as the driver climbed behind the wheel. "You're a good man, Blake Harper," she claimed quietly, her hazel eyes luminous behind her sexy glasses.

My throat clogged at the softness of her gaze and the sincerity in her voice.

"I promise to take advantage of every spa service they

offer." Her smile radiated like the sun, sweeping heat over me like the warm rays beating down on my head and shoulders.

She put up the window, and I stayed in place, watching her roll away, my heart full and chest aching.

Chapter 25

Wren

I'd always imagined a full body massage would leave a person boneless and empty minded. The first, I'd attained through the strong, capable hands of Loretta after an hour of kneading palms and fingers.

Pure. Heaven.

But my thoughts had refused the same rest. Even with the quiet, soothing music through the overhead speakers and the subtle scent of incense, my brain remained fixed on the conundrum of Blake Harper.

I'd thought I had him figured out, that he fit into a tidy box inside my mind where I could keep him safely tucked away from affecting my emotions, but he'd proved himself to be so much more.

Other stubborn people in my situation might have been offended by all he'd assumed to do in helping and taking charge, but I wouldn't ever look a gift horse in the mouth.

Especially after going above and beyond to bring me cupcakes, sing a song to me I hadn't heard since childhood, and hire a cleaning company to finish up the worst part of the task I'd cringed over having to do.

No one had ever spoiled me in such a way, and my heart had softened to the point of putty at the sweet warmth in his eyes any time our gazes happened to catch each other's while working.

Even though I had grief still roiling around inside my head and heart, desire had rested alongside throughout the entire time he'd been laboring in that shithole of an apartment complex to help ease my burden.

I'd felt his body's reaction to holding me, and I hadn't pulled away. Definitely hadn't been annoyed or wanted to roll my eyes either.

But he'd been a gentleman, hadn't tried to take advantage, and hadn't made one lewd or suggestive comment.

So maybe he had been honest in telling me he expected nothing in return.

I remembered the look on his face that night at Encore when I'd assumed he had been acting. I considered the expression, the vulnerability in his eyes earlier that morning when giving me the envelope.

No man was that good working off a script.

No possible way.

So why did a tiny part of me remain wary, evaluating every damn word and the lack of physical touch when I'd expected him to be a bit more handsy? Why did I look for a reason to keep him at arm's length even though he'd felt absolutely delicious pressed up against me when I'd hugged him?

He and I only had one person in common I could poke for information, so I made plans to do so once I was done being pampered to death.

After room service delivered stuffed lobster and a bottle of expensive white wine, both of which I would never splurge on for myself, I looked up my newest contact in my cell.

Madeline answered, and I settled back on the massive bed with its soft sheets and countless pillows.

"I heard someone got the birthday present of a lifetime," she said.

"I've never been so spoiled in my life," I admitted, smiling and not at all annoyed with Blake for spending so much money on me.

"My parents had gifted me a spa day there the morning of my wedding to Hudson. It was pure bliss."

"Every part of me is thoroughly relaxed except for my brain." I closed my eyes, expecting that once my thoughts quieted I would pass out for hours.

"What's on your mind, Wren?" Madeline asked as though understanding exactly why I'd called.

"Tell me everything you know about Blake."

She laughed lightly. "That's not much. I just met the boy last night when he showed up at our house asking for assistance."

"He and Colton have been friends for a long time?"

"Since high school," Madeline replied.

"Has he said anything about Blake?" I asked, desperate for information.

"Just that he's a great boss. Fair and faithful. Blake took us all out to dinner last night for helping you this morning."

A smile curved my lip. I wasn't surprised by his generosity. "Tell me everything."

"He and his friends enjoying teasing each other and laughing. There were a lot of work-related stories—typical guy stuff. They probably held back a bit with my being there though."

"How was Blake?"

"He seemed distracted, like his mind was on someone else." Madeline's voice held a hint of a smile. "And after how he'd behaved at our house on Saturday night, then this morning..."

"What?" I pushed when she trailed off.

"Blake is in love with you."

I snorted. "In lust, maybe."

"It's way more than that, Wren. He watched you all day today like you were the rising sun after a cold night in the dark."

I found myself stunned, wishing Madeline spoke the truth. "What makes you think that?" I whispered.

"Because I have two men who do the same with me, who would lay down their lives to save mine, would give up everything they own if it would bring a smile to my lips. Blake wants to make you happy, Wren."

He had and then some.

"Do you think it's...genuine desire though? I mean, considering his past," I tacked on. "He's known as a player. You should *see* his social media."

"Have you spoken with him? Outright asked him his intentions?"

My eyelids popped open. "Well, no." He'd always been pretty damn obvious in his actions...until after that day I'd cried in his arms. Things had changed that.

A shiver slid down my spine like a part of me had woken from a deep sleep.

"Honest communication is key in relationships—trust me on that one," Madeline said with a light laugh. "But friendships work the same too."

"I hinted at his gifts being given with the hope for something in return," I murmured.

"And what did he say?"

"He denied doing so, but that could also be part of his plan in getting me to go out with him. He's tried three times, and my stubbornness knows no bounds."

"Why have you told him no? Is it that you find him unattractive? Because I have to say, if you don't think that boy is hot as hell with a body worth climbing…"

I laughed. "Physically, he's a god, but that's not what I'm worried about."

"So what is holding you back?"

I considered Madeline's question asked with kindness rather than assumptions. "I'm too busy with school and the pharmacy."

"If two people want a relationship to work, they'll find a way. Even if your time together is only a few hours a week."

I chewed on the inside of my lip for a few seconds considering the bottom line of why he couldn't possibly want me. "What if he wakes up one morning and realizes that white trash doesn't belong in his world?"

"Excuse me?" Madeline actually sounded offended. "We are all humans. Period. No matter the color of our skin, our sexual orientation, our weight, height, or disabilities. We each have souls, hearts, and spirits. We are the same on the inside, regardless of our upbringing."

Madeline had a point, but not all people believed as she did.

"His parents wouldn't approve of me." I picked at a loose thread on the edge of the lily-white comforter.

"It's what Blake thinks of you that matters."

"What if I'm simply a challenge?"

"Wren." Madeline's stern voice stopped the questions from springing off my lips.

I closed my eyes and leaned back against the countless pillows atop the bed. "Hmm?"

"What will you lose by allowing Blake the chance to prove himself?"

"My heart," I answered honestly, thinking of all of Mom's guys who hadn't stuck around to even attempt being the daddy I'd never had. "That scares me more than anything."

"Would you rather live with regret?"

Her words stabbed into my chest, that feeling all too real and still tender. I had dozens of those with Mom. Countless words I wish I'd spoken. Conversations I should have pushed for and hadn't.

And now there's no chance...

Throat tight, I imagined spending the rest of my life alone, landing a good job, finally having some money once I paid my student loans off, but what did all that mean if I had no one to call my own?

I'd known loneliness almost all my life, but I longed for more. Someone to hold my hand. Buy me flowers. Write me love notes. Curl up with me in bed after a long day at work.

My body desired Blake, that wasn't a question.

"You have control over your future, Wren," Madeline stated, her voice as warm and encouraging as a mom's ought to be. "It's up to you to take what you want. Make things happen like Blake explained to us you've done with school."

"He told you about me?"

"Every other sentence out of his mouth last night while we were baking cupcakes held your name, and the look on his face was nothing but love. Believe me—I'm doubly well acquainted with the emotion."

I hardly knew Madeline, but I trusted what I had seen of her, Hudson, and Colton. Their affection, their easy way around each other, the lingering gazes I couldn't help but notice all morning long—and envying what they'd found.

Was it possible for me to experience that kind of love with a man so far above my station? Could I trust Blake had fallen for someone well outside his usual?

I wanted to believe.

And there *was* only one way to find out.

Skipping out on the next morning's spa appointments, I had the limo driver pick me up early and take me home.

Heart pounding, I kept my gaze off the condo jobsite behind me and focused on getting out of the limo and taking my bag to the stairs.

A note lay on my bottom step.

Wren,

I hope you enjoyed your night off and got some rest. Your mom's apartment has been cleaned and the keys delivered to the building owner, so you're free to focus on YOU now.

If you need me for anything, you know where to find me.
Love,
Your Hot Friend

I snorted even though my chest ached. "Arrogant asshole," I muttered, unable to help my grin.

Pulse kicking up, I tucked his note into my bag, rubbed my palms down my leggings, and turned.

The condo building's exterior appeared completed, the countless windows installed, manufacturer's stickers still in place. Construction workers milled around, but I didn't catch sight of Blake.

I filled my lungs and slowly let the exhale leak out in an attempt to calm my racing heart. No amount of measured breathing helped though.

My mind fixed on my future, I started across the street on shaking legs.

Finally ready to take a chance.

Chapter 26

Blake

"Wren's home early," Reid said, jerking my focus off the plans spread out over my desk.

The AC unit in the office window hummed in my ears as I glanced outside above it to see he spoke the truth.

Wren stood with her back to us, bag on her apartment stairs, my note in her hand.

She'd had a spa appointment that should have kept her at the hotel until close to noon.

My heart started thumping harder as worry settled into my gut. "I wonder what happened?"

She tucked the note away and turned before I finished speaking.

"Oh shit." Reid chuckled while I swallowed hard at the expression on her face.

Chin lifted, face flushed, she looked ready to march down a warpath. Sure enough, she started across the street.

But I didn't remember doing anything wrong...and that note had been nothing but kind. Or so I'd thought.

"Not sure if I should say good luck or enjoy." Reid

moved to let her in, while I muttered a curse at my best friend.

"I hope some woman grabs hold of your balls someday and squeezes until every breath you draw is only allowed by her mercy," I muttered, an adrenaline leak in my blood putting me on edge.

Reid barked a laugh and threw the office door open, letting in a burst of warm air and the sound of my men hard at work. "Hey, there beautiful!" he called, and I growled over his flirting with her.

I knew he did it to fuck with me, but still.

Wren's footsteps sounded on the metal stairs, and she came into view on the landing.

Fresh-faced, thick brown hair hanging around her shoulders, the sexy glasses perched on her small nose...she was so damn cute.

"Reid," she greeted him, "no offense, but get lost."

I bit my tongue to keep from laughing my ass off. My dick, however, kicked into lust mode at her commanding tone.

Reid looked over his shoulder at me, winked, and hurried down the stairs.

Wren took two more steps and stepped into the office.

The door clicked shut behind her.

The air between us sucked from the too small office, leaving me breathless. Or maybe it was the determined glint in her hazel-brown eyes that made me powerless to draw oxygen into my lungs.

"Wren," I rasped out her name, unsure of...everything, like I floundered in the deepest parts of the ocean without anything to hold.

Heavy silence settled as energy zapped through the distance between us. Every inch of my body vibrated, but I fought to stay still. Allowed her to make the move I hoped she planned on.

I swallowed hard, hands fisting at my sides. Waiting. Fucking *dying*.

"Blake, I—" She sprinted forward and slammed into me, those slender legs wrapping around my waist before I could blink.

My arms knew what to do before my brain processed her actions.

I grasped her small ass cheeks. They fit my palms perfectly as we stared at one another.

"I want you to make that fourth attempt," she whispered, her widened pupils full of vulnerability and hope. "Ask me out."

My heart pounded inside my rib cage "Are you going to turn me down?"

"No."

The *only* time I liked that answer on her lips.

Elation swept through me, and I lifted her ass higher so I could rest my forehead against hers. "Can I take you on a date, Wren Shipman?"

"Yes."

Fuck, that word... My dick bucked inside my pants, and I exhaled heavily, my eyes closing.

"Now ask me if you can kiss me," she whispered, her voice like a siren's song to every cell in my body.

"Fuck." Swallowing hard, I lifted my head to find a new gleam in her eyes. Playful Wren was going to wreck my world. "Can I taste your lips?" I asked what I'd been dreaming about since day one.

She shuddered, the black of her pupils growing larger. Releasing her grasp on one of my shoulders, she removed her glasses and leaned to the side to set them atop my desk.

Her focus landed on my mouth as she once more settled against me. "Yes."

I swooped in full force, set on devouring. Forget a gentle sampling. Too much pent-up desire lay on the edge of combustion inside me to take things slow.

Wren met me with equal hunger, her hands sliding into my hair to grab hold. Her lips parted, inviting me inside, and I licked into her mouth, a hint of cinnamon and coffee on her tongue.

Fucking delicious.

"Mmm," I hummed my pleasure over her sweetness, soaking in the wet warmth of her kiss.

She whimpered, wiggling in my hands, so I banded one arm beneath her ass, sliding the other up her back to grab a fistful of hair to keep her still.

Her deep moan filled my mouth—and I made note of that shit for future reference, because I'd found my newest addiction from a mere sip of her lips.

My toes attempted to curl in my steel-toe work boots. My heart pounded. And my aching dick...fucking hell, Wren turned me inside out from top to bottom. Every inch of my skin burned with the desire to feel hers writhing against mine. I wanted her sassy. Tired. Stubborn. Happy. Pissy.

Fuck, did I need every part of her.

Her panted exhales filled my lungs, and the slick, softness of her tongue caressing over mine thrummed need through my balls, drawing them up tight against my groin.

I would blow if we didn't slow shit to a simmer.

Twisting my hand to angle her head for better access, I tore my mouth from hers, loving how she released another one of those low moans.

My little birdie liked having her hair pulled.

"You should come over for coffee," she rasped as I detoured my kisses down her neck, fighting to keep my teeth in check. "Right. Fucking. Now."

I chuckled as my dick twitched in agreement, and I went back to her mouth to stop her from talking. The softest lips. The sweetest berry scent. The consuming *everything* about her drove me to the point of combustion.

But I longed to give Wren more than a quick fuck to ease our shared lust.

She deserved better than being bent over a desk the first time I sank into her.

It fucking hurt to back off, to untangle my tongue from hers, but being allowed the chance to thoroughly love on her body, I wanted full access. No time limit. I pressed a kiss to her cute little nose and held tight to her hair to hinder her from attacking me again.

She blinked, her pupils blown and lips red and puffy.

"You're so goddamn beautiful, little birdie."

I tilted her head to the side, angling her chin higher so I could slide my gaze over her pale neck. I imagined marking her there—holding her with my palm while fucking into her. Pre-cum smeared inside my pants.

"As much as I want to bend you over my desk and make you scream," I said, my tone ragged, "I'm not going to rush this."

Her brow furrowed, but I pressed a quick, chaste kiss to her parted lips to keep her from arguing.

"When I have the chance to strip you down again, have you all to myself, I'm going to take my time. Love on you so damn long and hard that you'll be boneless when I'm done. Exhausted. That okay with you?"

She licked over her lower lip, her eyes on mine and full of need. "I'm free right now."

"Friday night—if you aren't working?"

Her brow furrowed again. "I'm not, but it's only Monday!"

"Yeah. And?"

"You...you asshole!" She slapped my chest, and I laughed as she shimmied down my body, forcing me to drop my hold on her. She grabbed her glasses and slid them back into place. Hands on hips, she glared up at me. "Are you for real, Blake Harper?"

I studied her fiery eyes behind those sexy frames, loving her agitation, the fact she'd gotten so worked up for me. "I've waited this long for you Wren—I would wait for however long you changed your mind about needing me—"

"I want you *now*," she fumed, just shy of stomping her foot.

Another chuckle earned me a fist to the stomach I barely felt. "No."

She opened her mouth—and snapped it shut. Gaze narrowing, she studied me as though trying to dissect my brain for every thought residing inside. "You're getting back at me for turning you down all those times."

I stepped all up in her personal space, leaning my head down close to hers. Gaze dropping to my lips, she parted hers as though desperate for oxygen.

"I want to prove that I'm not only in this to satisfy my lust for you," I told her.

"I already believe that—"

"And I'm prolonging the agony so when I finally have the chance to sink into your body again," I murmured, "I don't have to worry about getting to work once we finish. I plan on taking my time, Wren. Worshiping every inch of you. Mapping out your skin with my fingers and tongue, which will probably be all night long."

A shiver ripped through her, and I zoomed in on the pulse thrumming in her neck.

"Gonna make you beg like you never have before. Cry for release." I lifted my focus to her eyes. "Then I'm going to work you over until you're a panting, spent mess, my name on your lips and your cum all over my cock."

"Your arrogance knows no bounds," she muttered, breathless for what I'd promised to do to her.

"Confidence," I corrected, straightening to my full height once more.

Our stare down lasted a few long, tense seconds. She wanted to demand action but showed more restraint than I'd expected after having finally given in to me. I'd seen the way she'd checked me out. I knew lust when I saw it.

"I need you to do something for me, Wren."

Her gaze turned wary. "What?"

"Save your next orgasm for me." Pink flushed her face, and I couldn't help but brush my knuckles over her warm cheek. "I'll make it worth your while."

Wren rolled her eyes, and I grasped her chin, squeezing her lips lightly until they plumped. I leaned down and licked over them. Nibbled. Sucked on the lower.

I wouldn't ever grow tired of tasting her sweetness.

"Four days of torture, little birdie," I whispered against her mouth, "then I promise to make you *very* happy."

She huffed. "If you don't deliver..."

Laughter erupted from me. She glowered as I dropped my hold on her and straightened. "You're adorable when you're pissy."

A heavy exhale eased her shoulders, her eyes losing some of their fire. Insecurities passed over her face like a shadow. "Why after all this time are you turning me down?"

I dropped to my knees, wrapping my arms solidly

around her, pulling her in tight against me. Doing so gave her the advantage of height to look down at me, but just barely. "I want you, Wren Shipman. You're not a conquest. Not just some mark on a bed post. You've captured my full focus. I haven't touched another woman since I met you. Haven't wanted or even looked at anyone. If you think I care about your past or even what you believe about yourself, you're sorely mistaken."

Wetness filled her eyes.

"Give me a chance to prove it? Let me show you how much you mean to me by making every second, every day, of what's starting here something special."

"Why me? I'm not fishing, I swear, Blake, but I don't belong in your world."

"You *are* in my world."

She rolled her eyes. "Anyone who catches sight of your Instagram account knows that's not true."

"I deleted it."

She blinked. "What?"

"That's not my life anymore," I said with a shrug. "The man I was before meeting the woman who turned me inside out is gone."

"I-I don't understand," she whispered, her eyes luminous behind those sexy glasses.

"Something about you..." I leaned up and brushed my lips over hers, a nerdy, cheesy as fuck one-liner coming to my mind. But fuck it. I wanted her to know every part of me in its entirety even though I'd told her I enjoyed sci-fi movies. "I'm caught in the tractor beam—you're pulling me in—and I'm not about to reverse thrust."

"Han Solo you are not," she said with a giggle, and fuck did I love that she got it and gave me Yoda in return.

"Nope." I pulled back and grinned, my heart ready to

burst from my chest. "I'm simply a boy on his knees before the girl I want to make smile every day."

She ran her hands through my hair, and I shifted my head to kiss her wrist. "Okay."

"Okay?"

Wren nodded. "Friday."

Chapter 27

Wren

The week took *forever* to pass.

I worked Tuesday through Thursday with Jenny, filling her in on everything that had happened Sunday after she'd left from helping with my mom's place.

And every morning, Blake sat on my bottom stairs, coffee and some sort of treat in hand to welcome me home. It was the kisses that made me smile though, soft and sweet, but I was ravenous for more.

I wanted his naked body on mine. In me. That confidence he portrayed took me to heights I'd never experienced before. During one of our long phone conversations through the week, I told him I had high expectations. He assured me he would meet them and then some.

We would see.

Settled once more into my usual shift, I expected I would be wide awake all night Friday, giving him that opportunity he'd said he wanted. To love on me until the sun rose. But secretly, I hoped he would fulfill his promises, and I would pass out with exhaustion from coming too hard and too much. My body was beyond primed and ready.

Who knew climax control could be so damn hot? My fingers itched to explore and bring relief countless times throughout the week, but I refrained because I wanted to gift him that release.

It wouldn't take much, that was for damned sure.

I felt like my libido traversed a tightrope, the tension and excitement barely tamped down from exploding.

But what brewed between us wasn't just about sex.

Our conversations over the phone and texts focused around getting to know each other. Our hopes and dreams, memories from our childhood, and a hundred other rapid-fire questions we took turns asking.

We discussed my grief, my regrets with Mom, and how he helped me cope with both by giving me something to look forward to.

Every ding of my cell made my heart race, the sight of his name on my screen welling up excitement and butter-flies in my belly.

I was like a girl with her first crush but with assurance that Blake actually liked me. Somehow, some way, the boy born with a silver spoon in his mouth found mousy little me attractive. Fun. Arousing.

While I didn't understand, I decided to take him at his word and trust he had thought of me as more than a conquest. Because even if I lost my heart, at least I wouldn't have to question the what ifs of never knowing.

Friday after work, I attempted to sleep but barely managed a few hours due to restless energy.

I had no idea what Blake planned for the night. The only thing I knew for certain was that we would end up in a bed eventually. Where, I had no clue nor did I care. As long as he fulfilled his prophecy of leaving me boneless and sated, I would be one satisfied woman.

I didn't want to appear too excited, but when he pulled up in front of my house, I grabbed my overnight bag he'd suggested I bring and headed out the door.

Blake stood at the foot of my stairs, head tipped back, a grin on his face.

My breath left in a rush. He was so damn fine, his focus on me like I hung the moon in his night sky just like Madeline had claimed.

Legs weak and chest giddy, I forced myself to walk down the stairs rather than fly and doubtless end up tripping head over heels until I landed at his feet.

I made it safely, my insides a jittery mess and my face hot.

"Hey, beautiful." Blake cupped my cheek, leaned in, and pressed his lips to mine. Firm and soft—and chaste, exactly as they'd been when he had welcomed me home from work earlier that morning before I'd attempted to sleep. "Ready for the night of your life?"

"Promises, promises," I muttered but couldn't help my wide smile.

He'd brought the truck and helped me into the passenger side, tucking my bag behind the seat.

While clicking myself in, I watched him round the front, adjusting himself with a slight grimace as though in pain.

Heat flushed through me at the knowledge I turned him on. Just the sight of me and a brief kiss had made him hard.

Had he denied himself orgasms all week too?

I found the thought arousing as hell and shifted on the seat to ease the ache in my core.

Blake climbed into the cab, filling the small area with

the scent of his soap and dryer sheets. Better than any expensive cologne he'd worn before.

"So where are we headed?" I asked, lacing my fingers atop my lap to keep them from showing him how nervous I was.

"To my boat." He started the truck and turned east to drive along the river.

"Seriously?" I angled on the seat to face him, my smile widening. I'd been to the beach but never on the open water.

"Yeah. My birthday present to myself last year. She's the love of my life, the only girl I've ever wanted to meet my parents."

Blake had told me he'd never been in a serious relationship before, but it sounded as though he'd never introduced a potential partner to his family. "You've never taken a girl home?"

"Nope."

"How many women have attempted to weasel their way into your heart to get that invite?" I couldn't help but ask, knowing the number had to be high as hell considering his name, his money, and how gorgeous he was.

"Everyone but you."

One of my eyebrows shot upward. "And how is that fact supposed to make me think you aren't only interested in conquering this mountain?" I asked, motioning over my body with my hand.

His intense gaze shivered over my skin. "I like you, Wren. Every little thing about you." He turned to face forward once more but didn't stop. "Your stubbornness. Your drive to better the circumstances you were born into. The fire in your eyes. The passion in your voice. The way you tilt your chin up in defiance and seem on the verge of stomping your foot when I say something to get under your skin. Your laughter is like sunlight. Your smile a rainbow after the storm."

I stared at his profile, my heart all aflutter. "How long did you practice that speech?"

"Wren," he groaned at my teasing.

"You're such a romantic," I murmured, completely blown away.

He shrugged, his cheeks pink. "Just speaking the truth."

Desire to climb onto his lap and kiss him senseless rose inside me, so I forced my attention on the road ahead.

"I've never been out on the ocean," I told him.

"You're going to love it."

"You're confident about everything, aren't you?" I asked, glancing over again to finding him grinning.

His flitting gaze caressed over my face. "Except for when it comes to you."

I unsettled Blake Harper.

"Oh?" I pushed because those words didn't sound real. How could they be?

He shook his head while navigating the rush hour rotary to continue along the river. "I'm thrown off my usual rhythm by you, Wren. You're like a splinter in my thumb I can't leave alone."

A small snort of air escaped my nose. "That, sir, is called the thrill of the chase."

He chuckled. "I look forward to proving your assumptions about me wrong."

"Considering what your social media used to portray..." I let the words trail off, shrugging.

"Stalker Wren."

"And why not? A hot construction worker across the street, his name plastered all over his truck. What woman wouldn't search your name and dive deep down that rabbit hole?"

"You think I'm hot."

I rolled my eyes. "Any warm-blooded female would ask Siri about half your crew."

"Have you?"

"Have I what?" I asked.

"Looked for any of my crew members on social media."

"I don't have names."

"You know Reid."

I bit back my smirk. "And don't forget Colton. Funny you didn't mention the man who's spoken for. Are you fishing for how I feel about your best friend?"

"I find myself strangely...possessive of you, Wren." He stated the words without a hint of suggestiveness or flirtation.

They were simply a fact that raced my heart and made me daydream about happily ever afters.

Chapter 28

Blake

We headed southward through gentle swells, my Whaler's outboard chugging us at a slow, leisurely pace.

Wren lounged on the seat beside me, head turning nonstop as if taking in every second of the new experience, from the shore on our right to the ocean meeting the horizon on our left.

"This was one of the things on my bucket list you know," she said, her eyes bright and her cheeks a gorgeous shade of pink.

She had told me over the phone earlier in the week which was why I'd chosen the event for our first official date. "Not getting sick are you?"

"No. This is..." she inhaled deeply, her smile growing, "absolutely wonderful. Growing up like I did, I never expected to enjoy an experience like this."

"The sad facts of your childhood don't make you trash, Wren."

"It did," she said, eyes still narrowed as though trying to figure out the one-liner I'd tossed out.

"Maybe to others when you were a kid."

She turned away, her focus on the ocean again. "It doesn't bother you to be taking someone like me out on a date?"

"Someone like you," he repeated. "Intelligent, beautiful, and sexy as hell? I'm one lucky bastard."

Her smile returned, her eyes dreamy.

"What are you thinking about, little birdie?"

"You and me," she admitted, shifting on the seat. "Or, rather, *me* in regards to *you*."

"Meaning?"

Her face flushed deeper, but she gave me her attention. "You step onto the road, and if you don't keep your feet, there's no knowing where—"

"—you might be swept off to," I finished for her, causing her jaw to drop.

"You did *not* just finish that quote," she sputtered.

"Oh, but I did."

"You...you *are* a total nerd! Oh my God!" She laughed, the sound a life-giving force rather than cringe-inducing embarrassment like Sara's had been.

I chuckled but didn't deny the truth.

Her gaze narrowed. "You're also a stuck-up, half-witted, scruffy-looking nerf herder."

I barked a laugh, so *goddamned* happy. "Only half-witted?"

She made a humphing noise. "Okay. One question I haven't asked you before."

"Shoot."

"Books or movies?"

"Books," I didn't hesitate to answer the truth no one on social media had known. "Every time."

"Oh my god," she breathed. "I may have completely misjudged you, Blake."

"So since you now know my deepest secrets to their fullest extent, back to that bucket list of yours," I said, slowing the engine.

One of her eyebrows shot upward. "What about it?"

"Any sexual fantasies other than the one Reid helped me check off for you?"

Heat rose to her cheeks, but she didn't answer.

"Picnic in the middle of the ocean?" I suggested. "Making out beneath the stars?"

"Sex below deck," she tacked on, rousing my semi I'd been sporting on and off all damn day.

"Why, Wren Shipman, are you propositioning me?"

"Just reminding you of your promises," she shot back, her sass doing nothing to calm my balls.

I wanted to yank her onto my lap and fuck her right out there in the open, but waiting, drawing out the anticipation would make release that much sweeter.

"I always keep my promises, little birdie, and trust me on this one—I've been dreaming about this night for too damn long."

The heat in her gaze took me to full mast.

We were going to be explosive, no fucking doubt.

I dropped anchor a few minutes later, my Whaler bobbing gently in the waves, the shore far enough away that no one would be able to see what we did without binoculars.

The sun had begun to lower as we got settled on the bow. I propped up the seat backs, and we lounged with the picnic basket I'd packed between us. Since I wasn't a cook, I'd picked up gourmet sandwiches and salads from my favorite bistro. I'd also brought along a bottle of white wine.

"To the night ahead," I said, lifting my glass.

Wren clinked hers against mine, and we held gazes while sipping, the energy between us rippling stronger than ever. Having tasted her mouth and having gotten to experience part of her body I had every intention of visiting again someday, I could barely restrain myself.

She called to me like a lure glinting in the sunlight. Irresistible, possibly fatal to my heart.

Wariness still crept into her gaze on occasion, but I was determined to gain her trust because I wanted to take Wren to meet my parents. I dreamed of tucking her against my side every night after she lay spent in my arms. I longed to hear her laughter, to see her smile every day. Feel her kisses whenever either of us walked through the door.

I wanted Wren.

Period.

"What are you thinking about?" she asked.

I popped the last bite of my sandwich between my lips and chewed, considering how honest I should be. Would she laugh at the truth, declare I only said such drivel to get into her panties?

Did she even wear any beneath that sundress?

Fuck.

I swallowed hard. "All sorts of good and naughty stuff."

"Oh?" She bit back a smirk.

"I'm wondering if you would give me a chance at more than one night and if you're wearing panties."

"More?" She focused on the first part of my semi-question.

"A lot of nights actually. Days too," I answered, watching her eyes go owl behind the lenses of her glasses.

She blinked. "You're...you want to *date* me? Like... boyfriend/girlfriend?"

"Yes." I decided to give her the truth because that was the only way things were going to work out between us. I'd been too damn fake for too damn long. If Wren wanted me, it had to be because she saw the man beneath the façade I'd worn for everyone but my family since high school.

"But—but what if we aren't compatible?" she asked. "What if the sex sucks?"

I barked a laugh, the tension from the moment easing off my shoulders. "Do you really think we aren't going to be like a solar flare, burning bright and hot?"

"What if it fades just as quickly?"

I studied her face as she lowered her gaze to the sandwich she'd only taken a few bites of.

"I could spend a lifetime learning the deepest parts of you and never grow tired or bored," I murmured.

Wetness hazed her eyes when she lifted her focus back to my face. "I'm nothing special."

My brow furrowed. "The fuck you aren't."

She sighed, glancing out over the ocean spreading endlessly on the horizon.

"You might not think that much of yourself, Wren," I said, "but you don't get to tell me how I see you. Understand?"

She swiped a tear off her cheek and nodded.

Although she hadn't agreed to be my girlfriend or told me if she'd worn panties, I decided to let both matters rest.

I wouldn't push on the first part. That ball lay in her court.

But the second? That answer I had every intention of learning long before the sun set.

"Now finish your sandwich so we can have some dessert," I told her.

"What do you have in that picnic basket?" she asked before taking another small bite of her sandwich.

"You told me your favorite fruit is strawberries, and mine is kiwi, so I brought some of both."

A few minutes later, I packed back up the leftover salad and half sandwich Wren hadn't eaten. We settled against the seat backs, picnic basket set aside, a second glass of wine in hand.

I popped open the fruit container and retrieved a strawberry, holding it out toward her.

Rather than taking it from my hand, she leaned in and bit into it, leaving half behind. Red juice smeared over her lower lip, and I zoned in on it while popping the rest of the berry between my fingers into my mouth.

The flick of her tongue over her lip tightened my groin.

"Next time, let me lick it off," I murmured.

A coy smirk lifted a corner of her lips. "Then feed me another."

Fuck, that sass on her tongue... She made my balls throb. Hard.

I held out another strawberry, and she repeated the action.

Dropping the other half into the container, I slid my hand around the back of her neck beneath her hair.

"Come here."

She gave in willingly, and I licked over her lower lip, tasting the tart sweetness of berries. Rather than dipping in for a deeper taste, I pressed a quick kiss to her mouth and moved back.

"Another?" I asked, already reaching for one.

"Mmm hmm," she murmured her agreement, her focus on my eyes the entire time.

Streaks of orange and gold split the darkening sky, but I

didn't want to wait for stars to shine down on us for the making out fantasy I'd asked her about.

I fed her two more strawberries, both times licking the juice from her soft, addictive lips.

"You're a tease," she muttered, her pupils blown, pulse thrumming in her neck.

"So *are* you?" I asked, ready for one answer, reaching my hand over to rub along her calf muscle.

"Am I what?"

I leaned in again, my face inches from hers while sliding my hand up over her knee. "Wearing panties?"

"No."

My dick bucked in its prison, and I groaned. "You're going to be the death of me."

Chapter 29

Wren

I'd known before heading out on our date that I would end up beneath Blake, and I hadn't been able to think about anything else the entire boat ride. Well, all week long really.

My skin burned for his touch, and every swipe of his tongue and chaste, soft kiss from his mouth roused me to the point I squirmed on the cushion beneath me.

I would be the death of him, he'd claimed.

A snort left me.

Quite the opposite, I wanted to state, but his hand sliding up beneath my dress along the outside of my thigh stole the words off my lips.

He set aside his empty wine glass as his palm grazed over my bare hip. Then he reached for mine and did the same.

"Come here, little birdie."

I couldn't even be mad at the annoying nickname... perhaps it wasn't so bad after all.

That large hand on my waist tugged, the other helping me along, settling me atop his lap. His cock lay hard and long beneath my core, but he didn't grind up into me like a horny jerk.

He slid his hand around to my bare backside, gently squeezing while the other tangled in my hair.

Spearing my fingers into his thick locks, mussing his hair beyond what the wind had done, I attacked his mouth.

I'd denied myself release all week long and hoped he had every intention of allowing me one climax before we went too far. It certainly wouldn't take much to get me there. I already skirted the edge, so damn turned on from denial that Blake would find a slick mess at the apex of my thighs as soon as he got around to touching me there.

Unable to help myself, I wiggled my hips while leaning in to bite his lower lip.

He groaned, tightening his hold in my hair. The slight sting only sent tingles straight to my clit, the slide of his tongue into my mouth intensifying the feeling.

We shared breath, both of us heightened by racing hearts and pure need to finally find fulfillment.

For endless hours, we kissed. Suckled on tongues and mouths, erasing the taste of berries and wine from each other. I roamed my hands down over his wide shoulders, over traps then pecs, mapping out the hard muscle that flexed as he did the same to me.

But not where I wanted him, where I burned for him.

I ground against his groin, knowing I smeared arousal all over his jeans, but he didn't seem to care, grasping my hips to help me along.

Finally—fucking finally, he moved beneath me, his hard length pressing against my aching core.

"You wet for me, Wren?"

"Soaked."

He made a low growling sound, his hands spanning my

waist beneath my dress, thumbs dipping low between my thighs. The pads of his fingers brushed over my pubis and trimmed hair, and I angled my pelvis to help him along.

A chuckle rumbled his chest. "Did you come this week?"

"No," I replied, breathless while shifting nonstop to get his thumbs where I wanted them.

"Good girl," he murmured.

A whine built up in my throat. "Blake..."

"Hmm?" he hummed against my ear, his lips plucking at my lobe.

I tilted my head, giving him complete access to my neck. "Please...I'm so turned on..." Swallowing hard, I once more attempted to manipulate where I needed his touch. "Make me come."

Blake nuzzled where my neck and shoulder met. "You want to make a mess on my lap?"

"Pretty sure I did already, but yes."

Another growl-like groan sent his heated exhale over my skin.

I shivered, goose bumps breaking out along my arms and legs. "Blake..." His name rasped past my lips, my voice pure need.

His thumbs reached down along my outer lips and back up, slick from my arousal.

"Fuck, Wren."

"Yes—yes, please," I gasped as he made the motion again, spreading me open to the coolness of the air.

The sky darkened overhead but I could still see where he touched me when I glanced down between our bodies.

"You need me here?" he murmured, one thumb moving inward to slide up over my entrance.

"Please."

"Mmm. Love it when you beg." He repeated the motion in an upward stroke but circled away from my throbbing clit. "So slick and hot."

"*Blake*," I whined his name, leaning in to capture his mouth again.

He met me with hunger, his tongue lashing between my lips to tangle with mine, his fingers continuing their teasing until I whimpered, yanking at his hair.

"Come for me," he whispered against my mouth, the pad of his thumb once more swiping upward through my folds.

I spasmed as he feathered over my clit. "Oh, shit."

"Right there, hmm?" He pressed and rubbed, sending a rush of heat over my entire body.

"Yes...oh yes!" Tingles erupted—and I came so damn hard my head tipped back, my moan choking on a gasp.

"Fuck, Wren." He groaned, his hold on my hips tightening and shifting me over his hard shaft.

Pure bliss shot through my core, clasping my pussy in tight pulses. A heady, lightweight feeling spread through my limbs, and I clung to his hair, gasping and whimpering over the emptiness inside me.

He sucked on my neck, a sweet, stinging pain as I came down, those damn thumbs of his rubbing in absent-like circles on either side of my sensitive clit.

I slumped against his chest, sagging against hard muscle and bone.

The musky scent of my cum and his soap mingled in my nose, a heady combination I didn't think I could ever get enough of.

"Better?" he murmured, sliding his lips up my neck to my ear.

I shuddered, my skin once more pebbling. "God, yes."

His huffed laughter caused me to shiver in his arms.

A full-on body sigh left my lungs.

Gentle waves rocked us. Salt-scented breeze ruffled my hair, tickling strands over my face. Lights twinkled in the distance, bringing the shoreline to life. The first stars sprinkled overhead.

I hadn't taken note of any of them since climbing onto the bow for our picnic. Blake had held me captive, all of my senses focused on him.

"Ready to head back in?" His voice rumbled beneath my ear, stabbing disappointment through my chest.

"Already?" I couldn't find the energy to lift my head off the heat of his hard chest.

"We had our picnic. Made out beneath the stars," he said, a smile lacing the words. "And my aching cock is so damn ready for that third thing you suggested I can't think straight."

"Sex below deck," I murmured as I remembered.

He barked a laugh as I scrambled off his lap, suddenly filled with energy again. Rather than moving with me, he watched me right my dress—and lifted his thumbs to his nose.

His deep inhale heated my skin, and I flushed, swallowing hard as he suckled them both clean. "So damn sweet, Wren. You're fucking delicious." The low timbre of his voice pebbled my nipples and pulsed an achy need through my core.

I squeezed my thighs together, staring at the obvious damp spot I'd made against the hard ridge inside his jeans.

"Let's go take care of that," I choked out the words, my mouth watering and pussy throbbing to be filled.

"Gonna dock first."

I groaned. "Seriously?"

"The waiting will make it that much better."

Grumbling, I set about helping to clean up our picnic, my entire body like a live wire, ants skittering over my skin and all.

Once underway, I sat on my seat and stared at his profile. The warm wind ruffled his hair, the dimmed lights of his...dash, or whatever you called it in a boat, cast warmth over his face, revealing pink cheeks. He licked over his lower lip and glanced at me.

"What's on your mind?" he asked.

"You're beautiful," I answered with the thought in my head. "But you're more than just a pretty face."

His slow smile melted my body a little more into the seat beneath me. "Am I?"

"You're thoughtful. Considerate. Compassionate. Kind."

"So you're saying I'm the whole package?"

I reached over to backhand his chest, and he laughed, grabbing hold of my wrist.

"Come here." Blake tugged, and I stood, squeaking as he spun me and sat me facing forward on his lap. "Want to drive?" he murmured against my ear, making me shiver. He placed my hands on the wheel and dropped his to my thighs. "Just hold her steady while I play with your sweet pussy."

"Shit," I muttered, my heart suddenly in my throat.

Blake didn't waste time. He simply rucked my skirt to my waist, his face diving into my neck as his hands reached between my thighs. He slid two fingers into me, and I gasped, biting my lip and shifting my hips forward.

"Mmm," he murmured. "So damn needy for my touch. I love it."

He rubbed deep inside me, thick fingers a nice stretch but not nearly enough.

I held the wheel in a death grip, staring at the shoreline, my pulse thrumming as Blake pumped his fingers in and out of my body, his teeth and lips nipping along my throat and clavicle.

"Gonna bury my face in here," he said, sliding his thick digits into me knuckle-deep. "Lap up your cream and swallow it down."

"Oh, God." I gulped, chasing after orgasm number two even though he ignored my clit.

"You want my tongue in you, Wren?"

"Yes."

"Want your sweet little nub between my lips?"

I damn near shot off his lap, whimpering my agreement as he brushed over my bundle of nerves.

"Soon, little birdie." He nipped my ear and slid his touch from my core.

My insides trembled with longing. Anticipation.

And the sound of his deep groan while sucking his fingers clean near my ear?

We couldn't dock that damn boat fast enough.

Chapter 30

Blake

My hands shook as I tied up my Whaler to the dock at the marina where I kept her.

I could feel Wren's gaze on me from where she stood at the stern, the need and connection like a live wire between us. Tension strung my muscles tight, and the state of my dick inside my jeans couldn't be pretty.

No doubt, a zipper imprint lay along my aching length. Pre-cum smeared over my sensitive head, making a mess in its prison. Hard as steel, my dick throbbed to sink deep inside her tight body.

She'd been so damn wet and slick. Hot. Sweet on my tongue.

Fuck.

I adjusted my junk, grimacing and telling myself to calm the fuck down before I blew like a teenager.

No woman had ever taken me to such an edge, where all I could think about was her coming undone around my dick. Watching her expressive face as she broke down, her core pulsing around me, her cries filling my ears. I needed to be the one to see her let go, swallow her moans and whimpers.

She stared up at me, her eyes wide behind her glasses as I gathered her hand in mine to lead her below deck.

We traversed the steep stairs without difficulty, the door shutting and leaving us in quiet. Our heavy breaths and the rustle of clothing sounded loud in my ears even though my heart pounded heavily alongside.

A couple steps took us through the salon into the cabin, low lights casting warm shadows over the light gray bedding and pillows on the bed taking up most of the space.

I turned just inside the pocket door, tugging Wren closer.

Her small hands landed on my chest, her eyes dark and luminous in the dim, golden light.

I removed her glasses and set them aside.

She kicked off her sandals while I did the same with mine, our gazes steady on each other's faces.

Sitting on the foot of the bed, I grasped her waist and pulled her in between my spread thighs. I slid my hands up the backs of her thighs, taking her dress along with me. Over the globes of her small, pert cheeks, up along her spine...that little sundress shifted willingly, baring her body to me.

"Want this off," I whispered, leaning back again to give me room.

Wren lifted her arms, and I worked the material up and over her head.

Lily-white skin...she stood completely bare from head to her feet.

I licked my lips as the dress fluttered to the floor.

A slight bruise marked her neck from my mouth filling me with a sense of proud ownership. The gentle swell of her small breasts and the dusky hue of her tight nipples made my teeth long to nibble. Taut belly...a slight flare of hips...dark trimmed hair at the apex of her thighs...my hands mapped them all. I could smell her arousal, a cloying musk that made my mouth water.

She was so tiny.

Perfect to maneuver.

I slid my arm around her waist, lifted her and then turned without effort, laying her on her back. Hair spread over the comforter, she peered at me with parted lips, a shiver sliding over her along with my gaze.

Planked on one arm, knee between her spread thighs, I leaned down to brush my nose over hers. "I can't wait to taste you."

She made a choking noise in the back of her throat, her hands finding my hair. I nosed down over her chin and neck, my lips leaving small kisses to the center of her chest. I nuzzled one breast, then the other, loving their sweet pertness, how the furled tip rubbed over my cheek.

Shifting back to stand, I chuckled when she cursed.

"I can keep my clothes on if you want," I said, pausing with my shirt's hem in hand.

"No—no. Take it off."

She swallowed audibly when I lifted my shirt over my head, and satisfaction coursed through my blood as she took in the sight of my bare chest. I'd been stared at before. Drooled over. But no woman had ever made me feel as wanted, as worthy, as Wren's hungry gaze set on devouring the sight of me.

I watched her study me, my every move, while unzipping and shoving down my jeans. Her eyes widened as she licked her lower lip.

Squeezing the base of my dick, I let out a soft groan, the anticipating of sinking between her thighs drawing my balls up way too fucking early. I hadn't lied about her killing me. I felt as though I hovered on the edge of a cliff, the past behind me, the deep reaches of the unknown far below.

I wanted so damn much with her. Everything. All her days, her nights—the restless, happy, and aggravated in-betweens.

"Can I have you, Wren?" I whispered, barely any tone to my voice.

"Yes." She replied without hesitation, but did she understand the meaning behind my question? The depth of my desire?

Letting the future rest in pursuit and enjoyment of the present, I went to my knees on the mattress, my hands beneath her tiny ass and my face right where I warned her I would go. I breathed in the sweetness of her, my nose sliding up through her swollen lower lips.

My tongue followed, and she jerked beneath me as I nipped at her clit.

"Holy shit," she gasped, her thighs clasping at my ears, her fingers once more in my hair.

"Mmm," I hummed my agreement and lifted her ass higher, diving into heaven.

Spearing my tongue into her tight clasp flooded my mouth with drool, and I lapped, swallowing down her sweet slickness. So. Goddamned. Delicious. I groaned and loved on her pussy with my lips and teeth, soaking in her whimpers and moans.

She panted, definitely on the edge of coming again, so I ignored her clit, using my tongue to explore every inch below, swallowing another rush of drool as I flicked over her pucker too.

"Blake," she moaned my name like a curse, her whimper

following along behind and making my dick buck between my thighs.

Fucking hell, this woman...

A full-on body tremor ripped through me, and unable to wait any longer, I sat back, shaking hands grasping at the condoms I'd left out earlier in the day. A few scattered to the floor in my haste.

Wren giggled. "Looks like someone has reached the end of his rope."

I grumbled a bit under my breath. She'd taken me past the point of control. I had to fucking have her.

Wren lay all spread eagle on my bed, panting, her stare on my shaking hands as I sheathed up.

My little birdie. Hungry for me—my dick.

Groaning, I bent down and licked through her wet slit again, dragging my tongue over her clit and pubis, her belly button...between her breasts, straight up to her mouth.

She wrapped her legs around my waist, and I sank into her body with one slow thrust.

Her back arched, her fingernails grasping at my shoulders as she gasped against my lips, a sense of euphoria rushing through me as though I'd swan dived off that damn cliff.

Ass flexed tight, I lifted my head and held still, the heat of her like a tight fist around my cock. I swallowed hard, drinking in the sight of her furrowed brow, the flush on her cheeks, the fluttering lashes as she blinked her eyes open.

Our gazes clashed, that tension I'd always felt between us so fucking intense my throat ached.

"You're perfect, Wren," I whispered while cradling her head in my hands. I had to bend at an awkward angle to reach her mouth, but I slid my tongue between her parted lips, needing inside her in every way.

She moaned as I shifted my hips, dragging my dick out of her pussy. Whimpering, she dug her heels into my ass to pull me back in. Not that I resisted. I slid forward with a groan, fucking into her mouth like I did her body, my backside tightening in attempts to reach deeper into her heat.

I wanted inside her soul. Wanted to fucking live there forever.

Our bodies moved in perfect rhythm, the wet sounds of her pussy around my thrusting dick, the noises falling from our lips the most erotic music I'd ever heard. The gentle rocking of the boat, her soft, warm skin beneath me, the heat of her exhales over my face...

Christ, I needed her.

I gave Wren everything I had stored up inside me, all the passion I'd never allowed a woman access to. Nothing held back, I laid it all at her feet, my heart included.

Chapter 31

Wren

Promises.

Blake had rained them over my ears countless times—and that boy delivered. I hadn't even come around his perfect dick, and I'd never been so overwhelmed with delicious feels.

He'd thrust in with one steady shove, filling me to the point I ached, the stretch around his girth creating a sweet sting I would remember for days. The slow roll of his hips, the gentle lashes of his tongue over mine sent me higher than I'd ever been with a guy before.

It was like our bodies spoke to each other, moving in perfect time without effort. Fluid grace. Waves steadily reaching for shore.

A connection I'd feared from the start seemed to wrap me up in a tight cocoon, offering life, emotional substance, to my touch-starved body. To my empty, lonely spirit that had gone without true appreciation since birth.

I rode the crest of shattering beneath Blake, my pulse thrumming and leaving me breathless with an intense need I'd never experienced during sex before. Every gyration of his hips ground his pelvis against my core, my arousal slick between us messy and noisy, but no embarrassment rose—especially when he moaned about how good I felt around his length.

"So wet," he whispered against my mouth. "Tight...so damn perfect, Wren."

A word he'd used to describe me before that I had brushed off as part of his scheme to get between my legs.

He'd gotten there and still insisted he found me as such. Twice.

I didn't understand. Couldn't. So I focused on the strength of him as he planked over me, the slick glide of his dick stroking in and out of me in a drugging, steady rhythm.

His shoulders flexed beneath my roaming hands, and I clung to the hard muscles along his spine, drinking in every grunt and moan from his lush mouth eating at mine.

Need...I needed more.

Whimpering, I squirmed beneath him, grasping at his body, desperate to sink inside him. Feel his warmth, know his mind. Touch and entwine with his soul.

Blake shifted upward, tearing his lips off mine. "Fuck, Wren..." Like he couldn't find words, he shook his head, his ass flexing beneath my heels as he continued to rock in and out of me, forehead furrowed and eyes clenched tight.

Sweat beaded on his forehead, and pink flushed his face. Lips parted, he panted and swallowed hard. "Wren," he whispered again, his eyelashes fluttering upward and navy blues catching my gaze.

My breath snagged at the desire, the longing in his darkened orbs.

Unguarded, he stared down at me with ten times the passion I'd seen in his eyes that morning when we'd woke face to face. His hands cradled my head with gentle warmth, his thumbs stroking over my jawline.

Lost.

That word summed up how I was beneath Blake but not in the way that caused fear. It was like he had swallowed up my ability to think, took control over my body and brain with sensory overload.

Him loving on me was all he had promised and more.

My throat went tight, and I fought to hold his gaze while overwhelmed, beyond ready for him to send me soaring. I wanted to come with him inside me. Needed to feel him thrusting through my spasming body. Longed to hear his groan as he joined me in bliss.

"Harder," I begged, lifting my hips to meet him.

He rested a knee on the mattress and snapped his hips, jabbing inside me.

"Oh, shit," I gasped, my eyes widening.

"Too much?"

"No—more."

A slow smirk curled his lips, and he gave me what I asked for, stabbing deep into my body. "Like this?"

"Yes—yes. Don't stop," I whimpered, lifting to meet his deep thrusts as he continued with an intensity that made my eyes roll back. "Fuck, yes. More. Please, Blake...need more."

Groaning at my begging, he wrapped his hand lightly around my throat.

"Oh, *fuck*," I croaked, tipping my head back to offer him better access while digging my heels into his ass.

"Yeah?"

"Yes," I hissed as he tightened his grip like I'd hoped for.

He rammed into me time and again as I tried like hell to dig furrows into his back with my blunt fingernails.

The slow, gentle grind lay behind us as we both gave way to our lust. The sound of slapping flesh took over our quiet gasps. Moans grew louder, curses starting to spill from both our lips.

"Feel so good, Wren." His harsh jabs slid me along the bed, and he released his hold on my neck to wind his arms beneath me, grasping my shoulders to keep me still. "Fucking hell."

I clung to his sweat-slickened hard body, biting into the top of his pec.

"Ah, *fuck.*" He rolled onto his back, easily taking me for the ride, his hands sliding down my sides to grasp my hips. "Ride me, baby."

I blinked, trying to center myself as he moved me over his dick back and forth, leaving me empty. Filling me completely.

Pushing upright, I straightened, making his length reaching deeper inside my channel. "Oh shit." I gasped as he thrust up against my womb, my eyelids slamming shut and abandoning me to darkness where my other senses took over.

Bruising fingertips dug into my hips.

The scent of soap and sex filled my nose.

Sloppy fucking sounds and panted breaths slid sensually into my ears.

Harsh strokes bumped against my sensitive cervix with just the right amount of pain it intensified the pleasure of having him inside me.

"Too much?" he asked without slowing down the pistoning of his hips. The slick glide of his hard length ratcheted up my need to come.

"Never." I dug my fingernails into his flexed pecs, making him hiss.

"Want you to come all over my dick." He panted. "Fuck, do I need you, Wren."

Whimpering, I leaned forward onto my hands beside his neck, my head hanging as he wrecked me.

"Look at me."

I forced my eyelids up, gasping for breath as our gazes clashed. That openness once more filled his eyes, sucking me into his soul...

"Goddamnit, Blake," I whimpered, grinding my clit over his pelvis, chasing release with abandon.

"Gonna come for me?"

"So hard. So *fucking* hard." A near sob ripped from me, and he lifted his head to meet me, taking my mouth in a kiss that lit my toes with tingles.

Blake bit down on my lower lip. "Come on my dick and take me with you," he growled, not losing his teeth's hold.

My climax slammed into me, ripping the air from my lungs on a shriek as I bucked against him.

"Oh fuck yeah." Blake banded his arms around me, squeezing me tight. His steady thrusts prolonged my climax, drawing out every sweet, rapturous rise and fall of bliss inside my mind.

I couldn't squirm, couldn't release the tremors attempting to ripple through me as my climax tried to shatter every cell in my body.

Blake lost control, his hips stuttering. A deep groan rumbled his chest against me, his dick bucking deep against my womb as I pulsed around his thick girth.

I wanted to feel the wet heat of his cum releasing inside me.

Over and over again.

Every. Damn. Day.

He grunted and slowed, releasing his tight grip on me.

A few aftershocks caused him to tremble beneath me as I went fully lax across his torso.

Every inch of my skin tingled in satiated euphoria. I rested my cheek on his chest and attempted to fill my lungs. Slow my heartbeat.

His thrummed beneath my ear, and I smiled, completely spent. Boneless. Mindless.

He rubbed down over my back with soothing caresses, squeezing my ass cheeks and attempting to stuff his semi fully back inside me.

I giggled.

"What?" He huffed. "I love how warm and tight you are around my dick. Could stay buried inside you for hours." He squeezed again, and finally went still beneath me. "Did I hurt you?"

"No." I expected him to be his usual arrogant self, wanting to hear all about how he'd kept his promises, but he didn't speak. Simply made quiet, satisfied noises inside his throat while trailing fingers over my heated skin in the most delicious act of affection I'd ever experienced.

Appreciation oozed from his touch, and I sank beneath the feeling like it was a warm blanket, finding the sweetest, most achingly delicious comfort.

I didn't feel the need to fill the silence, and neither did he. We simply...existed together as our hearts and breaths slowed. Eventually, he shifted me higher over his chest, his dick sliding free from my core.

I whimpered at the loss of connection between us.

He pressed his lips to mine in a soft, chaste kiss. "My shower is kind of small, but I want to take care of you."

Smiling, I kissed him again. "Okay." Groaning and rolling off him, I ended up sprawled on the bed. My entire body tingled with the afterglow of finally allowing Blake access to every inch of me like he'd been desperate for. Giving in had left me thoroughly loved up and satisfied.

He stumbled while climbing off the bed.

I giggled, my focus dropping to his ass as he entered the bathroom. So round and juicy. Made me want to take a bite.

The shower turned on, and I closed my eyes, slowly inhaling until my lungs reached the point of explosion as I luxuriated in a deeper sense of quietness than I'd experienced even during my hours spent in the spa.

No one had ever made me feel so relaxed, so—

A firm hand on my foot pulled my eyelids open and kept me from considering the warm fuzzies in my chest.

"Come here, little birdie." His dark blue eyes twinkled, his usual confident smirk back in place.

"You're criminal," I muttered, forcing my spent limbs to move.

"My dick?"

"All of you." I slid my feet to the floor, knowing I would have trouble holding myself upright.

"Is that a good thing?"

The hint of insecurity in his voice tilted my head back until our gazes latched together. Sure enough, he appeared unsure, the lack of confidence so damn endearing that my entire body ached to hold him close and run my fingers through his hair.

I didn't mind how he'd owned my body. Had stolen a part inside me no one had reached before.

"It's the best thing," I whispered up at him.

He leaned down and brushed his lips over mine in a slow, promising tease of a kiss. "I like you, Wren."

"I like you too, Blake."

Perhaps too much, but I strangely no longer feared that truth.

Blake lifted me into his arms as though I weighed no more than a feather and carried me into the cramped bathroom. With gentle hands, he washed and worshiped every inch of my skin beneath hot water and dimmed lights.

He made me feel treasured.

Chapter 32

Blake

I sensed Wren before I opened my eyes the next morning.

She clung to my body like a kitten seeking out warmth, all nuzzled against my side, arm over my chest, leg tucked between mine where I lay on my back. Her hot breath ghosted over my chest where her cheek rested.

Shifting my head to the side gave me a better view of her face in the early morning light shining through the east-facing window of the cabin. She slept, her lips still swollen from our kisses the night before.

Such a tiny thing, but she had taken every inch of me without complaint, asking for more, harder, loving how I held her neck with just enough pressure to raise her arousal to the next level.

She'd given me the green fucking light by offering her trust like that, and I had every intention of driving that damn car anytime she wanted. Even with her atop me, I'd been in charge, moving her body without effort, gliding her sweet pussy over my throbbing length.

I'd never come at the same time as any woman I'd slept

with. Had dreamed about it while watching the Renshaws. That couple had nothing on me and my little birdie. Fuck, the way Wren and I had looked at one another, the connection I could feel with her, was as real as the spunk I'd shot into the condom while she had pulsed around my dick.

My morning wood already poked the back of her knee, so I ran my hand over her thigh, pushing it down over my hips for me to grind against.

Wren sighed, and I wrapped my fingers up in her hair spread over my chest and bed, tilting her chin upward.

Her eyelids fluttered open, the slow, sensual smile curving her lips shooting lust straight to my balls.

"You're so beautiful," I said, my voice low and rasped from sleep.

"If you say so."

"Mmm." I slid her up my torso to reach her lips, pressing a soft kiss on them as both my hands wrapped in her long hair. "I do."

She rubbed her nose over mine, shifting to climb aboard my body again. Her sitting and wiggling landed my hard cock up along her ass crack.

My hands fell from her hair to grasp her thighs.

She ran her fingers over my upper body, mapping out my shoulders and pecs, slowly dipping over my abs. A whispered sigh escaped her lips.

"What?" I couldn't help but ask, expecting my smirk appeared cocky as fuck.

She backhanded my left pec. "You know what."

"I think you need to tell me."

"And what? Inflate your ego even more?"

"Nah." I shook my head, loving the sass glinting in her eyes. "I just need to hear how hot you think I am."

"Need or want?" she asked, arching a brow, her finger-tips trailing over the V of my hips.

My dick jerked, bumping up along her crack, and my stomach muscles contracted at her teasing touch.

"Need *and* want. No one has ever made me feel the way you do, Wren."

Her smile faded as our gazes locked, and her hands stilled atop my lower abs. "I'm afraid to ask."

"Don't be," I murmured, running my hands up her thighs in soothing caresses.

"I'm...I'm not ready for anything more right now."

Her words dug into my chest like a damn knife, but I wasn't surprised. She faced a final year of schooling, a full load of classes while working night shift four days out of the week. She would barely have time to breathe let alone live it up with a new, insatiable boyfriend.

"I know," I forced myself to say in acceptance, reaching up to cup her cheek.

She sat silent atop me, her thumbs rubbing absently over my stomach. Lower lip between her teeth, she studied my face. Searching.

And I let her see it all. Whatever the fuck she wanted, I held nothing back from her probing gaze.

"You aren't going to sit back and wait for me to finish school, are you?" she finally spoke.

"I'm not going to stop *being here for you*," I promised so she knew how I'd taken her opinion. There was no question, not when it came to me possibly moving on. "I'll leave you notes. Show up when you least expect it to spoil your exhausted body and mind rotten. Yes, you've got a lot on our plate starting in two weeks, but I'm going to weasel my way into your life without you being aware...until you're expecting to see me. Thrilled to have me all up in your space. Begging me to be your personal escort, available at your beck and call."

She snorted. "I'll admit you were so damn good last night that I'd gladly pay for another couple of hours in your bed."

Ego. Swollen.

"Then let's not waste time, little birdie," I said with a grin, but she slid over my thighs and between them before I went to roll her onto her back beneath me.

Sprawling out onto her belly, she held my gaze, those hazel-brown eyes of her luminous and hungry. She nuzzled my ball sack, and I groaned, my hands finding her hair as I spread my legs wide to give her full access to whatever part of me she wanted to explore.

Biting the inside of my lip, I kept from begging her wandering lips and flicking tongue to take me deep.

She tongued my taint. Suckled on first one ball then the second.

"Fuck," I groaned, my abs going tight.

No woman had ever worshiped my entire package. Blow jobs, yeah, but Wren took her time, loving on every inch of my groin until my heart raced. Lapping at my balls. Nipping at my taint. Even licking over my hole...

"Wren—baby—please. Fucking *hell*, woman."

She hummed her pleasure while sucking my left nut and popping off. Sass lit in her eyes as she dragged her tongue up the back of my shaft.

"Christ." I swallowed hard as she grasped my base with her small hand, her soft touch pulling my dick upright from the small puddle of pre-cum it had rested atop. More oozed from my slit, leaking down the side.

She swiped it clean with her tongue, another hum of approval tightening my nuts.

"You're killing me," I muttered, sure I dreamed.

Her eyes alight, she held my gaze and took me into her mouth, her lips caressing down over the fingers attempting to span my girth near my base.

Hissing, I fought to hold still, allowed her to love on my body with unselfish attention, sucking and licking, driving me *fucking* insane.

"Gonna come if you don't stop," I stated through gritted teeth, not sure if she was ready for a mouthful or wanted to bounce on my dick.

She pulled free and ran her fist up over my sensitive head, milking another droplet of pre-cum to bead on the tip. Holding my gaze, she licked it away, shoving her tongue into my slit.

"I want it." Down went her open mouth, and my hips lifted on their own, fucking into her throat and gagging her.

"Shit—fuck, Wren, I'm sorry."

She moaned, her free hand trailing down between her thighs to get herself off while blowing me.

"Fuck." I swallowed hard and slid deep into her throat again.

She gagged a second time, and another moan leaked around my cock.

"Relax, baby," I crooned, my thumbs on her hollowed cheeks as she sucked upward. "Let me in deeper—want to shoot my load right into your belly."

Wren shuddered and sank back over my length.

I pushed upward, holding her head in place, my dick down her throat.

"Jesus," I groaned out the word as she shuddered, the tremors I'd seen the night before as she came.

I allowed her breath and a moment to cry out her release—and slid right back into the tight heat of her. My balls erupted, shooting hot spurts of cum down her throat. She choked and swallowed around my head, and I cursed up a blue fucking streak, gently fucking my balls dry over her tongue.

She lapped and sucked until I went boneless, gasping oxygen into my starving lungs as she did the same.

"Goddamn, Wren, that was... Shit." I choked on a chuckle, an arm falling over my face.

She kissed her way up my abs.

Bit my damn nipple.

"Fuck!" I jolted beneath her, and she snickered, suckling the pain away. "Get up here, woman," I growled, yanking her up over my body and claiming her mouth.

Fuck morning breath.

Fuck the fact her tongue tasted like my spunk.

I wasn't ever going to get enough of her.

Chapter 33

Wren

Two weeks until classes started.

Fourteen days of sleep Blake insisted I take advantage of whenever he wasn't inside my body or spoiling me with lavish dinners at expensive restaurants. Twice more, we went out on the boat and made out beneath the stars. He slept over at my apartment on the nights I didn't work, gladly—proudly—taking that walk of non-shame across the street to his jobsite.

Every morning he left me, I watched him through my kitchen window while sipping coffee.

Blake Harper was nothing like I'd assumed. Every hour I spent with him, he shattered my preconceptions and made me fall just a little bit harder.

I knew things would be different once classes started. My free time...I wouldn't *have* any. Couldn't afford any distractions that would affect my grades and scholarships.

I'd warned him countless times, but he would kiss my words away and murmur he wasn't going anywhere.

He stood beside my shitty car to see me off to my first

class, offering a hard hug, a quick peck, and encouragement to kick ass and enjoy my day.

I did, excitement to sprint that final straightaway to graduation filling me with focused determination to finish strong. How and when I would see Blake, I didn't know, and I found myself...wishing for more hours. Perhaps one extra day on the weekends, because what budding relationship could survive on Sundays alone?

Would he grow bored of waiting to spend time with me?

He had the sexual prowess of a damn bunny, always willing and ready to love on me and give me the physical attention I craved, so would the sudden halt to a weekly romp in the sheets keep him engaged?

My chest ached at the thought he might decide it wasn't enough—*I* wasn't enough, that I would once more be without the physical touch I couldn't get enough of.

I exited my last class of the afternoon, my bag weighed down with notebooks, papers, and a couple of books. I'd asked off work for the first day, knowing I would be mentally exhausted.

Eyes stinging from the lack of sleep I'd gotten the night before thanks to Blake, I stumbled down the building's stairs.

"Hey, little birdie."

My focus jerked up off the walkway leading to the parking lot.

Blake leaned against a maple tree a few feet away, a single rose in his hand.

Warmth rushed through me, settling in my cheeks. "What are you doing here?" I asked as I moved closer to him with a spring in my step that hadn't been there the moment before.

He straightened and tugged me in with his free hand,

landing a lingering, soft kiss on my lips. "Congrats on finishing the first day of the final leg."

Laughing lightly, I kissed him again. "Thanks."

He took my bag and handed me the flower.

I sniffed the sweetness deep into my lungs. "You know what red roses stand for," I murmured without glancing up at his face.

Blake wound his arm around my back and started us up the path. "I do."

I didn't push, and he didn't offer any words until we stopped beside my car. He opened my passenger door and ushered me in before climbing behind the wheel.

"Wait," I said, my brow furrowing. "How did you get here? Where's your truck?"

"It's a surprise." He backed out of the parking spot, keeping his focus on where he drove.

"What's a surprise?" I asked, having no clue what he had planned. We hadn't discussed anything other than my calling him later that night after I collapsed on the couch to decompress.

"I'm taking you out for dinner—"

"Blake."

"—and we'll keep it short. Promise. I know you're tired, but..."

"But what?" I pushed.

He laced his fingers atop mine on my thigh, glancing over at me. "Do you trust me?"

I raised an eyebrow and stared at him, my eyes giving him all my pissy sauciness and then some.

"Shit." He chuckled and shifted on the driver seat.

A quick glance at his groin told me why he'd done so.

Smiling sweetly, I squeezed his hand. "You like me sassy."

"Fucking love it," he groaned the words. "Damnit, Wren."

I laughed and faced forward, holding his hand and sniffing the rose he'd given me.

"Two hours," he stated firmly, "then I promise to have you home so you can do whatever studying you need to. I'm not staying over. Won't keep you up all night long."

I sighed, wishing he could.

"But I'm bringing Dunks in the morning before work."

He slowed in front of a huge house, parking in the circular driveway.

I shot him a look.

He winked. "Come on."

Hopping from my car, he acted like a little kid, rushing around the hood to get to me before I could open my own door.

Hand on my lower back, he led me around the side of the house and through a black iron gate. Fancy gardens spread across the backyard in full bloom, filling the air with a sweet fragrance.

"Blake?" I asked, completely baffled.

"Trust me, baby." He steered us toward the right onto a cobbled pathway toward a wooden awning that had green vines climbing its posts.

Three people sat at a table beneath.

Oh shit.

I swallowed hard at the sight of Blake in silver fox form —from the wide shoulders to the same navy-blue eyes.

A beautiful blonde woman stood along with him, and a younger version of her flashed pearly whites as she grinned at me from the far side of the table.

The blood drained from my face, and in that moment, I

knew he'd been intentional in giving me that rose, knowing *exactly* what it stood for.

My throat tightened, and I swallowed down threatening tears. "What did you do, Blake?" I whispered, my stomach tightening.

Blake tugged on my arm, pulling me forward when I hadn't realized I'd stumbled to a stop. "I brought you home to meet my parents who just got back from Florida, little birdie."

Both of them smiled at me without a hint of prejudice in their eyes as I processed his words and what they meant for him.

And me.

Before my thoughts went any further, his sister moved around the table with a squeal and threw herself at me. Like Blake, she towered over my slight frame and could very well pass for one of those models stomping down a runway.

She hugged me close, hand rubbing my back, all while laughing as I struggled to accept what was going on. "I'm *so* excited to meet you!" she gushed, wiggling me back and forth like we were long-lost best buds.

Something I'd never had.

Tongue-tied, I hoped my smile didn't tremble as she stepped back, still holding my arm.

"I'm Brenda, the bratty baby sister—yes the alliteration is on purpose, and it's all Blake's doing." Her smile dazzled. "I've heard so much about you. You have no idea. I even know *your* nickname. Little birdie. It's so sweet!"

I glanced up at Blake.

Cheeks pink, he shrugged. "Dad, Mom, this is Wren," he said, what sounded like pride lacing his voice as he slid his arm around my waist.

"Hello, dear," his mother said, hugging me the same as Brenda had.

She was so damn welcoming that tears filled my eyes, and I had to bite the inside of my lip to gain control of myself. Like Madeline, Mrs. Harper felt like a mom should. Warm and soft, her hugs full of comfort and affection.

Mr. Harper clasped my hand between both of his, those familiar eyes twinkling, the flirt. His slow smile melted me, easing the tightness in my throat. I knew where Blake's ability to make the ladies swoon had come from.

As his family returned to their seats, I tugged Blake's sleeve and crooked a finger. "Why did you do this?" I whispered as he leaned down.

He straightened again, his face serious, eyes peering into mine as he cupped my cheek. "Because you're it for me, Wren."

A tear slid from my eye, which he brushed away with his thumb.

"You've bewitched me body and soul."

I choked on a laugh through my tears. "You did *not* just say that."

His wink sent flutters through my stomach as he pulled out a chair for me.

"So Blake tells us you grew up in Lynn, Lynn, the City of Sin," his father recited the hated rhyme, those eyes of his still twinkling as he reached for the glass of white wine in front of him.

So much for the flutters—and what a way to start off the dinner conversation. My entire body clenched up, my face heating and chin lifting, all those good feels from seconds before gone in a flash of harsh lightning. "Yes. I was born and raised in Lynn. My mother was a prostitute and drug addict."

His smile turned even warmer. "I never knew my dad, and I lived in the worst slums of Lynn until I turned eighteen and made my own way in life."

My breath left in a rush. I slumped back in my chair, staring for a few seconds, processing what the older version of a very wealthy Blake had claimed. He'd been white trash once upon a time too.

I glanced over at Blake's mom. "And what did your father think about you dating a boy from Lynn?"

Her lips twitched as she glanced over at her husband. Their hands entwined atop the table. "Daddy hated him and said he wasn't good enough for me."

I wasn't surprised—but I *was* at their being together all those years later.

"What changed his mind?" I asked, my voice small. Hopeful as hell.

"I told Daddy that I'd found the love of my life, and nothing on heaven or in hell would change my mind. I then gave him the option of accepting the man I loved as-is or losing his only daughter."

My eyes widened. "You didn't."

"Oh, I definitely did." She winked.

Mr. Harper lifted their clasped hands and kissed her knuckles.

Blake reached beneath the table and caressed my knee, the heat of his hand searing me through my pants.

I clasped mine atop his and squeezed tight.

"I hear you're a complete geek like Blake," Brenda said, drawing my gaze and my focus off all the bubbling happiness wanting to erupt inside me. "You'll have to come to Comic Con with us this year."

A half laugh escaped me.

"I always go as Galadriel," Brenda said.

"Of course you do," I replied, easily seeing her as the elfin princess.

Brenda studied my face. "You'd make a great Princess Leia. Oh!" She glanced over at Blake. "You'll have to give up Boba Fett and be Han Solo this year!"

I snorted with laughter, my insides jittery. "He's cocky enough to fit the roll."

"So you'll go?" Brenda asked, leaning forward with her elbows on the table regardless of the salad atop her plate.

Steeling myself, I turned toward Blake.

Heat and a whole lot of...something else filled his eyes, speeding up my pulse.

"Yeah, I think I will," I whispered, fully giving into the draw of his tractor beam.

"Well, I for one am thrilled that Blake has finally brought a woman to meet us," his mother said, breaking the achingly sweet tension between me and her only son.

"It's about damn time too." His father lifted his wine glass, and we all followed suit, my pulse fluttering and mouth trembling with a smile. "To the young lady who has stolen Blake's heart." His eyes overflowed with acceptance like I imagined a loving father's might be. "Welcome to the family, Wren."

Forget holding back the tears. One leaked down each cheek, but I quickly swiped them away, my heart so full I couldn't keep from smiling.

Chapter 34

Blake

W ren hung on my arm as we walked out to my car exactly two hours later as promised. Her face glowed in the setting sun, her eyes bright and happy. My sister had claimed her as her newest best friend, begging to meet for coffee or lunch before she and our parents flew back down to Florida the following week.

My chest had swelled with elation when Wren had agreed.

And after Dad's toast and watching him and Mom hug Wren goodbye with assurances to see each other again for the holidays...

Yeah.

I'd definitely brought the right woman home to meet them.

"I don't want this night to end," I said and kissed her temple, breathing in the scent of sweet berries as we ambled back through the gate.

"I have a much cheaper bottle of wine in my fridge than the one we shared with your family," Wren stated with a more than suggestive invite in her voice.

"Perfect." Grinning, I shut her into the car and jogged around to climb in and be close to her again. "So did you like your surprise," I asked, "or was it too much too soon?"

"Dinner couldn't have been more perfect. Your parents are...lovely."

"I'm a lucky kid."

"You're going to be even luckier in about an hour."

"Oh?" I shot a glance over to find her face flushed. "Now I'm intrigued."

I tore out of my parents circular dive as fast as Wren's car would go, making her giggle. She put her hand on my thigh, and my cock pressed against my fly.

All throughout dinner, I'd imagined taking off her glasses, ripping her clothes off her body and physically claiming what my mind already had.

Her roaming fingers moved up my thigh as I sped up the highway, and I tipped my hips toward her hand as she grasped my length. She squeezed, drawing a groan from me.

"Keep that up, and I'll be useless for an hour at least," I stated, not really ready for her to stop.

"Well." She withdrew her fingers and folded her hands on her lap, making me curse in protest. "We can't have that now, can we?"

"I want to sink into your pussy with nothing between us," I blurted. My dick and balls throbbed at the thought of taking her bare. "I got tested after my last hookup, but if you'd rather not—"

"Yes," she interrupted, her tone breathless. "I want to feel you too, Blake. Skin on skin. Fantasized about it that first night on the boat."

I cursed and adjusted my hard dick. "Are you on birth control?" I asked. "Because the last thing I want to do right now is get you pregnant—we'll save that for a few years after graduation when you're all settled in as head pharmacist somewhere."

Silence filled the car, and I glanced over to find her wide eyes unblinking as she stared at me.

"Too much too soon?" I asked again, my voice low and so damn hopeful she'd reply with a big, firm *no*. Fuck knew I'd thrown a lot of not so subtle hints about how I felt for her.

"I-I don't know what to say, Blake."

I grabbed her hand and kissed her knuckles like Dad always did with Mom, forcing my focus back on the road. "I told you I'm not going anywhere. Even if I only get to see you on Sundays, even if we have to skip a weekend here and there, you're not getting rid of me."

"Well okay then."

Another glance revealed her soft smile and the kind of longing in a woman's eyes that made a man's knees go weak.

"I've fallen for you so damn hard, Wren. You came in like a damn nor'easter and knocked me off the fake foundation I'd built my life on. You make me want to better myself. *Be* myself, the person I don't let too many people see."

She didn't reply, and I had to take an exit before I could look her way.

Tears filled her eyes, and my stomach went all tense and shit.

"Wren? Talk to me. Please," I pleaded, my entire future I'd envisioned with her suddenly feeling as though it skated on thin ice, ready to crack beneath me with whatever thoughts filled her mind.

"I tried so damn hard not to want you or even like you," Wren said as I pulled into her parking spot in front of the old Victorian.

"But?" I pushed, while turning to face her, my hands shaking.

She scrambled over the console and wiggled onto my lap, her small palms pressing against my cheeks. "Resistance has been futile."

A corner of my lip curled upward at the Star Trek reference I'd thought after first meeting her. "In that case…"

I pushed open the door and climbed out with her in my arms, not bothering with her bag. Bypassing the step I'd often sat on while waiting for her—wishing and praying for a chance—I took her up the stairs, skipping every other one.

She buried her face in my neck and sighed. "I love our size difference and how you carry me around like I weigh nothing."

"I love doing it." I bent over to retrieve the extra key she hid behind a crack in the door casing.

I let us into her apartment but didn't put her down. "I haven't taken you against the door yet," I murmured, pushing her back against it once I closed us inside. "Been thinking about it though."

"Then do it," she whispered, yanking on my hair.

I crushed my mouth to hers on a moan. Adrenaline rushed through me, causing my heartbeat to race. I pulled her hair as her fingernails sank into my traps. We fought for control like two squalling cats, hissing, sweet pain flaring beneath each touch.

"I want to fuck you in half," I said, grinding my cock against her softness.

"I'd like to see you try." She gasped as I set her on her feet and yanked her pants and panties straight to the floor.

My mouth found her slit to make sure she was ready for me, and her hands went to my hair.

I slid one of her shoes from her foot while licking up through her folds, and she kicked off her pants from that leg.

"Good enough," she whispered. "Hurry."

I quickly stood, freeing my dick. Leaning in, I took her mouth again, winding one arm beneath her bare knee. I hitched her up against the door, settling her leg around my waist.

Keeping our mouths fused together, I thrust balls deep into her slick sheath.

"Oh fuck...fucking hell, Wren. You feel so good." I groaned into her mouth, holding still in her tight heat. "Never been inside a woman bare before. Christ."

Wren wiggled in my arms, her other leg clamping around my waist. "You're so hot. Hard. My God, do I love this."

One arm under her ass, the other hand tangled in her hair, I pulled her head back until she flinched. While dim in the apartment, I could make out the details of her face in the streetlight coming through the kitchen window. Eyes wide and focused on mine, her lips parted as she panted for breath.

"You feel so fucking perfect clamped around me," I said, my mouth dragging along her jaw. She whimpered, trying to move against me, but I held her still. Arms tight around her, I sank my teeth into her shoulder.

She shivered against me, and I pulled out to the tip before slamming her against the wall again. With each thrust, she groaned, fingernails digging into my scalp. I rammed into her, fighting for control to keep from splitting her body in two.

"Harder, Blake, fuck me harder."

Could the woman be any more perfect?

Involuntary grunts with each mad thrust ripped from

me as I gave my little birdie exactly what she wanted, pounding into her again and again, the slap of our skin obscenely loud in the quiet apartment.

"Want you to cream all over my cock, Wren," I told her, my mouth resting against hers as we panted together. "Need to feel you squeeze the living hell out of my dick. Send me over the edge, baby, so I can fill you up with my cum."

"Oh God." She gulped, her back arching.

"Yeah, give it to me," I rasped, watching her face as she fell apart.

A shriek ripped from her lips, and I pumped harder, drawing every last spasm from her body as her cum oozed over my drawn up balls.

Jaw clenched, I forced myself to stop before erupting. Wren sagged in my arms, her eyes closed.

I kicked off my shoes and stepped out of the pants that had fallen around my ankles, arms starting to tremble from the adrenaline crash and holding her up. Still buried deep and clasping her close against me, I strode into the bedroom.

"You're going to give me another one," I said lifting her away from me and flipping her over onto the bed.

She giggled while getting onto her knees and wiggling her pert little ass.

"Christ, woman." I grasped her hips to keep her still and thrust into her dripping pussy.

She cried out as I plunged deep, hitting her womb. "Blake! Holy...*fucking* shit!"

Twisting my fingers in her hair, I pulled her head back, yanking with each piston of my hips. Sweat soaked through my shirt as my balls slapped against her, the musky scent and wet sounds of our fucking driving me toward the looming cliff, one I wanted to swan dive off of every day for the rest of my life.

I tugged harder on her hair, lifting her body upward until she sat on my lap, her back against my chest. Grinding into her and teeth nipping her neck, I ran my hand up her thigh, fingers reaching for where I impaled her. Wetness seeped from her swollen lips, and her protruding clit hardened with need. I pinched, and a sharply drawn breath arched her against me.

"Need you to come one more time for me," I said, thrusting deep and pinching again.

A tremor rippled through her, and she cried out, her pussy squeezing me like a vise.

Giving over, I slammed into her with abandon, hollering her name as I erupted deep inside her body.

"Shit, baby." I gasped for air, my lips against the top of her head as one last shudder tore through me. "I'm officially dead."

She giggled, and I squeezed her tight, wishing I could stay lodged inside her body forever.

Chapter 35

Wren

I sprawled on my back, cum leaking between my legs. Exhausted and beyond caring, I didn't shift to shimmy out of my shirt shoved up beneath my armpits or rid myself of the bra one of my breasts had escaped.

Blake knelt between my spread thighs, running a hand down his heaving chest atop his T-shirt. "Need water," he croaked, his voice low and raspy.

I sighed, shutting my eyes. "I'll grab us some in a minute."

"Did I wear you out?" He caressed up my thigh.

I swore the man couldn't keep his hands off me—not that I minded in the least. I craved it with an unsatiable hunger. "Mmm. Maybe just a little."

"Can't say I'm sorry," he said, his voice betraying a smile.

I couldn't help my grin. "I'm sure you're not."

"Did I hurt you? You asked for harder, but..."

I took stock of my limp muscles and tingling scalp. "I'm fine. You?"

"Just dying of thirst."

With a groan, I rolled to the edge of the bed and stood on jelly-like legs. Shuffling and cum dripping down my thigh, I made it to the bathroom. Pink flushed my cheeks, and my eyes sparkled back at me in the mirror as I washed my hands after emptying my bladder.

Blake had put that sated, happy look on my face, one I'd never seen before.

Falling or fallen, I accepted the fact that I was truly deep into...something with the man I'd thought to be an untamable playboy. Madeline and Hudson had done it with Colton from what I'd heard, so why couldn't Blake change his ways too?

Still smiling, I went into the kitchen to grab two glasses of water.

Blake lounged on my bed when I came back, gloriously naked, sexy bedroom eyes taking me in from head to toe.

"Lose the shirt."

Arousal lit again, warming me through. I handed him both glasses of water and attempted a striptease, slowly pulling my shirt off overhead and twirling it around while shimmying my hips. Seeing as how I'd never done that sort of dance before, I felt like an idiot, but the flames that licked at me from Blake's heated gaze changed my mind.

The shirt whispered down to the floor. I flicked open my bra I'd tucked my wayward breast back inside and pulled the straps down my arms to let it fall free.

Blake sipped his water, gaze glued to my hard nipples. Although his cock remained flaccid, I climbed onto the bed and straddled his hips. He handed me my glass, and I settled onto his warm skin, rubbing my damp core against the trimmed hair of his pelvis.

"Ready for round two?" I asked, a bit breathless.

A smirk appeared on his luscious lips as he palmed one of my hipbones. "This is when having Reid along for the ride is worth the intrusion."

I tsked, narrowing my gaze. "Naughty boy."

His lips flatlined, his eyes losing all trace of teasing. "I've never claimed to be an angel. There's tons of shit in my past, Wren, but I promise to be true to you if you'll have me."

I sipped, the water cool sliding down my throat. "So you're saying you'll be an angel from here on out?"

"Yes."

"Hmm." I pretended to think about his declaration. "Well, I happen to enjoy your darker side. The whole choking me thing and pulling my hair. Fucking me against doors. What if I want more of it?"

His pupils dilated. "I'll be whatever you desire, Wren. *When*ever."

I lifted my drink and smiled over the rim. "And if I'm thinking about another round with a third wheel?"

A slight furrow appeared between his eyes.

I'd caught the hints of jealousy he'd portrayed whenever Reid got handsy with me and had asked only to tease him.

"Say the word and we're yours to use as you will," Blake finally said.

"You would really share me now that we're together?"

He rubbed his thumb over my hip bone in gentle circles. "If that's what you want."

I took a big swallow of water, my face going hot. "You're more than enough man to fulfill me, Blake Harper. I'd rather it just be us."

He released a heavy exhale as though he'd been holding his breath and I hadn't noticed. He pushed some hair over my shoulder, and his fingertips trailed down my chest, lingering to roll a nipple while I drank down the rest of my cold water.

"I'm in love with you, little birdie," he murmured, those navy blues latching onto my eyes as his hand landed on my waist.

A few drops of water flew past my lips as I coughed and set the empty glass on the bed stand beside us. He'd hinted...but I hadn't actually believed...

"C-come again?" I gasped.

"Mmm." His damn smirk... "It'll be at least another fifteen minutes or so before I can do that."

I smacked his chest.

The teasing light in his eyes faded, but the warmth remained. "We haven't known each other long, but the connection I feel with you—it's like nothing I've experienced before. Hell." He huffed a quiet laugh. "I took you home to meet the parents. I'd say I'm pretty well gone on you, Wren."

I settled again on his lap, studying his face for any trace of bullshit and found none. That bubbling of hope and happiness rose one more inside my chest. "So your father welcoming me to the family...how did he know?"

Blake caressed up my neck to cup my cheek, his eyes intense and full of that damn emotion I hadn't yet named out loud in my head even though he'd spoken the words. "I told him how to toast. I wanted to see your reaction. Get some sense of where your heart was and if you'd be open to accepting the fact you owned mine."

Well, damn. Tears hazed my vision.

He wrapped his hand around my neck and pulled me close, resting his forehead against mine. "I hope you'll think of my family as yours in time," he whispered, "because you deserve to have a loving mother and father. Even a bratty pain-in-the-ass sister."

I laughed a little through my tears, and Blake shifted back to lick them off my cheeks. Without asking for an answer or my thoughts, he moved his lips to mine for a lingering kiss. My heartbeat sped as his cock thickened beneath me, but our kiss remained slow and leisurely, full of shared emotion.

Releasing a heavy sigh, Blake pulled away, searching my eyes.

I couldn't help my smile as the perfect line popped into my head to answer the question I could see wanting to escape from his heart.

I clasped my hands to his cheeks so he didn't look away. "I would rather share one lifetime with you than face all the ages of this world alone."

"Nerd." He laughed but squeezed me tight.

"Takes one to know one," I sassed, shifting my hips against the hard length pressing between my thighs. "Now, lose the water so your fingertips can bruise my hips again, Blake."

"That mouth of yours..."

"Send me to bed sated, and I'll wrap my lips around your delicious cock in the morning."

"Fuck." He swallowed hard and shifted my hips, lifting me slightly so the tip of his dick pressed against my opening. "I'm going to love you so damn hard that I'll have to carry you into the shower and hold you up while washing you."

I rested my forearms over his shoulders and pressed my chest to his, my lips a breath away from his. "Promises, promises."

He pulled me down, stuffing me full.

We both moaned.

"Wren." He licked over my lower lip and clamped an arm around my waist to keep me pinned to his body. "I can't think of a cheesy line to fit this moment, but some poet needs to put to words what I'm feeling right now."

I smoothed back his hair, smiling. "Your thoughts out loud would be better than someone else's, Blake."

"I'm overwhelmed with appreciation." His lips didn't curl upward, and the seriousness in his eyes faded my smile.

I touched the tip of my finger to his lips.

He nipped, then kissed me there.

"Head over heels never held meaning until I got to know you," he whispered. "You're a breath of fresh air. Honest and kind. You aren't interested in my name or wallet. You like *me*—nerd, geek...whatever you want to call me."

I squeezed my inner walls around his girth, and his eyes rolled back into his head.

"Wren," he groaned.

"Don't stop now," I whispered against his ear, shifting enough that his dick dragged along my inner walls.

"Shit." He grasped my hips, pulling me back onto him fully. "This sweet little body...so lithe and perfect. It took four attempts, but you're finally mine."

"Oh am I?" I asked, threading my fingers through his hair, unable to keep a teasing smirk off my lips while lifting and lowering my core over his hard shaft.

"Yes, Wren. You're my little birdie for life."

Warmth rushed up through me, creating a sweet ache in my chest. "In nine months, I'll graduate and we can begin our forever."

"Fuck that. You're moving in with me next week—hell, tomorrow—so I can make you dinner, help you study...I'm even going to pack your lunches and do your laundry."

I snickered. "So damn confident." I tsked, still working his dick with my body. "Might want to rephrase that statement into a question to make sure that's what I want."

Blake grasped my hips, stilling me. "Please move in with me, Wren. Let me be the happiest man on the planet."

"Well." I kissed his lips, drawing out the moment and making him wait just a little longer. "I *do* love it when you beg...in fact, I just might love you too."

"Wren." He dragged out my name with the cutest whine.

"Yes, Blake."

He took my mouth—or rather, I gave it willingly, same as I planned to do for the countless days ahead of us in a future full of family, affection, and love.

All of which I had missed out on.

Until him.

THE END

About the Author

USA Today bestselling author Lynn Burke is a CrossFit and coffee addict. Her three spawn and two fur babies dictate how often she can be found hunched over her Mac, typing as fast as her fickle muse cooks up hot stories.

You can find more about Lynn at her website: www.authorlynnburke.com

Also By Lynn Burke

Abel's Obsession

Divulging Secrets

Healing Storms

In Between

Reluctant Lumberjack

Resisting his Mate

Billion Dollar Love Anthology

Blood Born Series

Bonds of Worship Series

Dark Leopards MC

Darkest Desires Series

Devil's Outlaws MC

Elite Escort Series

Elite Escorts MM Series

Fallen Gliders MC

Forbidden Obsession Duet

Found by Fate Series

Midnight Sun Series

Missing Link Series

Risso Family Series

Sandy Ridge Series

Sinful Nature Series

Vicious Vipers MC